M000266863

Tripped Out

Also From Lorelei James

Mastered Series – Erotic Romance
BOUND
UNWOUND
SCHOOLED (digital only novella)
UNRAVELED
CAGED

Need You Series – Contemporary Romance
WHAT YOU NEED
JUST WHAT I NEEDED
ALL YOU NEED
WHEN I NEED YOU

Single Title Novels
RUNNING WITH THE DEVIL – Erotic Suspense
DIRTY DEEDS – Contemporary Romance

Wild West Boys Series – Contemporary Romance
MISTRESS CHRISTMAS (novella)
MISS FIRECRACKER (novella)

Single Title Novellas
LOST IN YOU (short novella) – Contemporary Romance
WICKED GARDEN – Erotic Romance
BALLROOM BLITZ – Contemporary Romance

Mystery Novels Written As Lori Armstrong

Julie Collins Series – Private Eye Mystery
BLOOD TIES
HALLOWED GROUND
SHALLOW GRAVE
SNOW BLIND
DEAD FLOWERS (novella)
BAITED (novella)

Mercy Gunderson Series – Army Sniper/Native American Mystery
NO MERCY
MERCY KILL
MERCILESS
DOUBLE SHOT OF MERCY – Short Stories coming fall 2017

Tripped Out

A Blacktop Cowboys® Novella

By Lorelei James

1001 Dark Nights

EVIL EYE
CONCEPTS

Tripped Out
A Blacktop Cowboys® Novella
By Lorelei James

1001 Dark Nights
Copyright 2017 LJLA, LLC
ISBN: 978-1-945920-39-4

Foreword: Copyright 2014 M. J. Rose
Published by Evil Eye Concepts, Incorporated

All rights reserved. No part of this book may be reproduced, scanned, or distributed in any printed or electronic form without permission. Please do not participate in or encourage piracy of copyrighted materials in violation of the author's rights.

This is a work of fiction. Names, places, characters and incidents are the product of the author's imagination and are fictitious. Any resemblance to actual persons, living or dead, events or establishments is solely coincidental.

Acknowledgments from the Author

Huge thanks to Goldie from City Sessions in Denver, for setting up a fantastic personalized cannabis tour, led by Matthew, her knowledgeable and (patient!) associate. More thanks go to the folks at The Herbal Cure, for allowing us to experience their amazing grow house (Josh, your plant knowledge blew me away) and for the expertise of their budtenders in the totally chill dispensary. Thanks also to the Pure Dispensary for showing us the industrial side of CO_2 extraction and the wide variety of THC & CBD infused products on both the medical and recreational sides. You ALL are truly ambassadors for the positive aspects of the legalized cannabis industry in Colorado.

That said, any errors (or artistic license I took) in this fictional story are solely on me...

As always, to THE Liz Berry...you inspire me with your generosity and I thank the universe every day that I get to call you a friend ☺

To Evil Eye—Liz and MJ Rose—so thrilled I got to be here another year!

Sign up for the 1001 Dark Nights Newsletter
and be entered to win a Tiffany Key necklace.

There's a contest every month!

Go to www.1001DarkNights.com to subscribe.

As a bonus, all subscribers will receive a free
1001 Dark Nights story
The First Night
by Lexi Blake & M.J. Rose

One Thousand and One Dark Nights

Once upon a time, in the future…

I was a student fascinated with stories and learning.
I studied philosophy, poetry, history, the occult, and
the art and science of love and magic. I had a vast
library at my father's home and collected thousands
of volumes of fantastic tales.

I learned all about ancient races and bygone
times. About myths and legends and dreams of all
people through the millennium. And the more I read
the stronger my imagination grew until I discovered
that I was able to travel into the stories… to actually
become part of them.

I wish I could say that I listened to my teacher
and respected my gift, as I ought to have. If I had, I
would not be telling you this tale now.
But I was foolhardy and confused, showing off
with bravery.

One afternoon, curious about the myth of the
Arabian Nights, I traveled back to ancient Persia to
see for myself if it was true that every day Shahryar
(Persian: شهريار, "king") married a new virgin, and then
sent yesterday's wife to be beheaded. It was written
and I had read, that by the time he met Scheherazade,
the vizier's daughter, he'd killed one thousand
women.

Something went wrong with my efforts. I arrived
in the midst of the story and somehow exchanged
places with Scheherazade – a phenomena that had
never occurred before and that still to this day, I
cannot explain.

Now I am trapped in that ancient past. I have taken on Scheherazade's life and the only way I can protect myself and stay alive is to do what she did to protect herself and stay alive.

Every night the King calls for me and listens as I spin tales. And when the evening ends and dawn breaks, I stop at a point that leaves him breathless and yearning for more. And so the King spares my life for one more day, so that he might hear the rest of my dark tale.

As soon as I finish a story... I begin a new one... like the one that you, dear reader, have before you now.

Prologue

Liam Argent, age sixteen...

Lurking in the shadows of buildings, wearing a black hoodie, jumping every time a siren sounded in the distance...yeah, he was some cool customer, all right.

Ain't like this is your first drug buy, Argent.

As if his conscience needed to remind him of that fun factoid.

Liam checked his calculator watch for the tenth time. Pointless, really. Dealers ran on their own schedule. When they said "Be there at ten," it meant be there between nine and eleven o'clock. A few times, his source "Junior"—likely not even his real name—hadn't shown up at all. His excuse was "family obligations."

He swung his arms a couple of times to keep warm, which caused his coat to ride up his forearms, exposing his skin to the frigid night air. He'd grown four inches since last winter and now his coat didn't fit. He hadn't mentioned it to Gramma because she'd feel guilty that a new coat wasn't in the budget for this month. He'd have to make do. Like he always did.

A Gran Torino pulled up to the curb. Liam waited, not sure if it was Junior since he never drove the same car twice.

The passenger window rolled down. Junior motioned for Liam to get in—all while the car kept inching along.

Liam didn't hesitate, not even when his common sense screamed at him not to get into a drug dealer's vehicle.

Ain't my first drug buy, remember? he said snarkily to his conscience to shut it up.

The interior of the car reeked of clove cigarettes and bleach. Liam held his hands in front of the vents blasting out hot air, grateful for the warmth as he waited for Junior to speak first.

"Kid," Junior said as he picked up speed and turned onto Hawthorne, "where are your gloves?"

"I...ah...left them at school."

Junior harrumphed as if he didn't believe him.

They kept driving until Junior found a spot he saw as safe to make the exchange. He threw the car in PARK and left the motor running.

Liam dug in the front pocket of his jeans and pulled out a crumpled wad of cash. Even the damp paper smelled of stale grease, courtesy of the restaurant where he worked. He cleared his throat. "Look, I'm ten bucks short. So, can I owe you ten next time? I promise I'm good for it. Or do you want to cut ten bucks' worth out of the bag?"

Junior took the money and smoothed each bill out before shuffling them from the highest denomination to the lowest. Without looking up from his ritual, he said, "I ain't the bank, letting you run a line of credit, kid."

Liam said nothing.

"Nor am I in the bidness of dividing bags I already parceled out." Then Junior looked him in the eye. "What's your deal, boy? I get a message from you every two weeks. Always the same amount of product. No more, no less." He gave Liam a head-to-toe once-over and frowned. "You ain't got the desperate look of a full-time user, although that coat has seen better days."

Liam remained mum.

"The dope ain't for you, is it?"

"You warned me from the start that you didn't want to know details about my life and shit," Liam reminded him.

Junior shrugged. "Humor me."

He said humor like *yumor*—not bothering to mask his Jersey accent.

"My gramma suffers from chronic arthritic pain. She can't afford the pain pills or any other type of treatment. This stuff works."

"Has she asked for that synthetic kind, what's it called—Marinol?—that's legal?"

He shook his head. "It's still too much money. Your product is way cheaper." Wait. Had he just insulted a drug dealer? "And way better," he added.

"She gives you money for this?" Junior demanded.

"Some. I kick in the rest from my restaurant job. That's why I'm short on funds this time because my hours got cut."

"But Granny knows you're buying her meds on the street?"

"It's 'don't ask, don't tell' with us." He glanced away, hoping Junior wouldn't see the lie. "She's taken care of me since I was five. So when I do this, I feel like I'm taking care of her."

"Jesus. You really are the wholesome kid you appear to be. Honesty is a rarity in my bidness. You wouldn't believe the lies people will tell to get their next fix."

Liam bristled. "I'm not scamming you. This *is* for my gramma. I don't—"

"Inhale?" Junior said on a laugh. "Just jokin' with ya." He lit a cigarette and studied Liam through the smoke. "Your hours got cut, huh? So you're lookin' for more work?"

"Yeah."

"How old are you?"

"Sixteen."

"I could use a kid like you to make a couple of deliveries for me a week."

Don't even consider going to work for a drug dealer!

Again, Liam told his conscience to shut up and boldly said, "I'm listening."

"Smart of you not to say no right off the bat and hear me out."

Liam swallowed hard. What if Junior wouldn't give him a choice?

"You'd be…shall we call it…a courier," Junior continued, "taking package A to location B. Maybe eight hours a week total. Maybe a few more."

"Why me?" he blurted out.

"For one thing, you ain't a user so I don't gotta worry you're gonna fuck me over because you're jonesing for a fix and start stealing dope from me." Junior puffed on his cigarette. "The other thing…a geeky, glasses-wearing kid who looks like a damn Boy Scout ain't gonna raise suspicions. People will smile at you and believe you're just out doing more good deeds."

For the first time ever being a nerdy brainiac might pay off. "How much does it pay?"

"Depends on how far you gotta take the package across town. I'd guess it'd be around two hundred a week to start. And to sweeten the deal, I'll discount Granny's biweekly weed order by twenty percent."

Holy shit. A reduced price for Gramma's medicine and double the money he earned bussing tables? Fewer hours meant he could thoroughly research his options for college scholarships and get his applications in early.

"One time offer, kid. What's it gonna be?"

"I'm in as long as I can be out as soon as I turn eighteen."

Junior flashed his teeth. "Good to see you ain't such a pushover. But bear in mind, there's risk. If you get caught while couriering said packages, I expect you to play that innocent Boy Scout card."

Liam offered his hand. "You got yourself a deal."

* * * *

Stirling Gradsky, age sixteen...

"Jesus, Stirling. Pull the stick out of your ass, stop being such a damn goody-goody, and take a hit. It's not that big of a deal."

Stirling Gradsky glared at her older sister London, then at the joint London brought to her mouth and inhaled from.

Again.

London held the smoke in for several moments and blew it out. Then she smiled and cocked her head, sending her long auburn hair cascading over her shoulder.

Resentment surfaced. Her older sister had the charisma that made boys and men want to gather around her. London was carefree, rebellious, sometimes reckless, but it all came naturally to her. After a full day of trail riding in the dust and muck, London looked beautiful. The glow from the campfire had her hair shining like spun copper. Even with that old, holey, smelly horse blanket draped around her shoulders, she managed to look both elegant and wild.

Stirling pulled her own blanket tighter, hoping London would forget about her and return to flirting with the cowboys surrounding the campfire.

But London wouldn't let it go. "Come on. Drop the holier-than-thou attitude, baby sis, and try some." London shoved the joint in Stirling's face.

She managed to bite out, "No, thank you."

London's eyes narrowed. "What is your problem?"

"Besides the fact that what you're doing is illegal?" she snapped. "I prefer to have all of my brain cells intact. Apparently that doesn't matter to any of you."

Laughter rippled around them.

"Or are you afraid you'll get the joint stuck in your braces?" London said with a snicker.

That mean comment just made Stirling angrier. "Maybe I'm concerned about germs. I don't want to put my lips on that thing when I don't know where any of *their* lips"—her derisive gaze encompassed the group of four guys and one other girl—"have been."

"God. You are such a pain," London complained. "Why are you even here if you don't want to have a little fun?" She took another drag, locking her eyes to Stirling's. "Oh, right, Mom *made* me take you."

A wave of heat washed over her. She hated how much her sister had changed in the last year since she'd graduated from high school and started running wild with the rodeo crowd. London had no time for her anymore. So Stirling had begged their mom to make London take her on this trip, hoping they'd have some time together to talk, even if it was at night in their shared tent. But London had brought her own pup tent, leaving Stirling to bunk alone. And Stirling wasn't stupid; she'd heard her sister's giggles and groans coming from one of the guys' tents the very first night.

So this trip sucked, even before everyone started getting high.

"Stop naggin' her." The guy next to London snagged the joint, took a big drag, held it in, and blew it out. "That just means there's more for us."

Dale, the good-looking cowboy on London's other side, had his turn with the joint. "Man. That is some good shit," he said on a long exhale.

Everyone murmured their agreement.

Then they were all laughing about something dumb that one of their friends had done—a guy Stirling didn't know—so she literally sat there like a bump on a log.

An invisible bump on a log.

Story of her sixteen-year existence. She knew she was awkward. She also knew it wasn't a "stage," as her mother had assured her. No. This was the real her—the socially inept, brainy geek with goals beyond getting baked every weekend.

"Hey, I'm at the end of this joint," Lizzie said. "What do I do?"

"Give it here." London pulled a bobby pin from her hair and skillfully turned it into a roach clip, which just proved this wasn't her first go-round with weed.

When the laughter gave way to singing, Stirling had had enough. She slowly stood, wincing at the muscles screaming in her back, legs, and arms from spending hours on horseback. Just another reminder that she had ambitions beyond working in the family horse breeding and cattle business. She dreamed of a job where she could wear silk blouses and sky-high heels, not boots and jeans.

No one noticed her leave.

In her tent, she buried her head in her sleeping bag, trying to block out the animal howling contest the stoners started when the coyotes began their nightly yowling. She felt a little smug when a collective paranoia set in that maybe the coyotes would bring the wolves in closer and they all scattered to their tents.

Or maybe they all had a bad case of the munchies.

Stirling snorted. No wonder they used to call it reefer madness.

Then she promised herself to steer clear of marijuana forever, no matter what.

Chapter One

The first rule of being a prankster?

A killer poker face.

And Stirling Gradsky had that down pat.

The second rule of being a prankster?

Learn your opponent's weak spots.

Maybe Stirling didn't have that rule down entirely. Her pranking prey, Dr. Liam Argent, remained as much a mystery now as he'd been when he'd waltzed into High Society ten months ago and declared himself emperor.

Okay, maybe not emperor, but he definitely acted like the laboratory was his private kingdom.

His appearance hadn't been a surprise. Stirling's brother Macon, her business partner in High Society—a cannabis operation that included a retail store, a medical dispensary, and an onsite grow house—had informed her that he'd hired a guy from California, a cannabis expert, to work in the lab.

After dealing in euphemisms regarding all things cannabis related, Stirling believed "the lab" was Macon's shorthand for the grow house. She imagined the California dude to be an older version of the iconic stoner character Spicoli from *Fast Times at Ridgemont High*.

Turned out she had been wrong on both accounts.

Macon had indeed meant he'd created a full-blown, state of the art laboratory, complete with a beefed up security system for their resident cannabis expert. And the "dude from California" turned out to be Dr. Liam Argent, stuffed shirt extraordinaire, with advanced degrees up the wazoo.

The man drove her crazy.

Crazy.

From day one he'd refused to tell her what he was working on in his fancy-ass lab. When she'd complained to Macon about Dr. Argent's secretive manner, he'd instructed her to leave Dr. Argent alone.

Her brother may as well have waved a red flag in front of her.

She'd tried being friendly…to no avail.

She'd tried being bossy…to no avail.

She'd tried every "employee relations improvement" tactic she'd learned in her years in the corporate world…to no avail.

Hence her oh-so-mature decision to prank him until he cracked. She'd worked with men like him before. At least if you got them angry enough, they'd yell at you, which nine times out of ten led to an actual conversation.

Except Dr. Argent hadn't shown the slightest chink in his armor. In fact, he'd joined in on her prankfest and one-upped her on occasion.

Which was why today's prank ranked as one of the better ones he'd pulled on her.

It was also why Stirling was massively annoyed.

Her assistant Shanna said, "Stop huffing around. You brought this on yourself because of the feud you and Dr. Argent are currently engaged in."

"I have no idea what you're talking about."

Shanna rolled her eyes. "Right. This is his retaliation for you leaving him a message to call Mike Hunt last week."

Stirling snickered. "Come on. Having him call a gynecologist's office asking for Mike Hunt was classic. The only person who didn't see the humor in it was Dr. Tight Ass."

"I recognize that demonic look, boss," Shanna accused. "You're already planning payback."

"Or maybe I'll do nothing. Him waiting and worrying when I'll strike next will freak him the fuck out."

"You wish. The man is an enigma. A *hot* enigma."

"Did I hear you say he needs an enema?" Stirling retorted.

"Omigod, you are impossible. I'm probably wasting my breath, but I'll ask you to please consider ending this feud."

Shanna was probably right. Stirling should take the high road.

But where was the fun in that? And although she'd never, ever, *ever* admit it to anyone, this back and forth she had with Argent was the most fun she'd had at work in years.

"Anyway, now that you've done your duty giving the Weed Worshipers the tour of Mecca, what's next for them? They're waiting."

"I've got a special surprise lined up."

Shanna shook her head. "Oh no. Please tell me you're not planning—"

Stirling whirled around and forced a smile on her group. "For the divine intervention that brought you to the tour today, you'll receive twenty-five percent off purchases in the retail store."

That started an excited buzz.

Please don't start genuflecting again. The minute the Weed Worshipers had seen the thousands of plants in full flower, buds heavily coated in sticky crystals, two weeks from harvest, they'd fallen to their knees like true believers.

"And no tour would be complete without visiting our state-of-the-art lab, run by our very own mad scientist. A man who works behind the scenes to build better buds for the whole world."

The Weed Worshipers whispered among themselves.

"I have a favor to ask of all of you. Today is our scientist's first day back to work after successfully kicking his sexual addiction. He hasn't made whoopee with his blow-up doll for a full week. So could we sing him a chorus of 'He's a Jolly High Fellow' to show support for his struggle?"

Jeff, the Minister of Marijuana, the head...*head* of spreading the good word about weed, stepped forward. "For he who fills our coffers, it'd be our honor, ma'am."

"Great! Follow me."

Normally the back section of the facility was restricted. She escorted her group down a narrow hallway, pausing with her keycard in hand at the laboratory's glass door. She flashed back to the time Dr. Asshat had restricted her access to his lab—by installing an electric shock device on the door handle. The longer she touched it, the stronger the current. The man taunted her by holding up a sign that said BUZZ OFF from behind the window beside the main door.

He could get her riled up like no one else she'd ever met.

She swiped the card and the green light flashed.

Stirling led her charges into the mad scientist's domain. *Mad* being the operative word.

The instant her nemesis appeared she felt that roiling drop in her stomach.

No denying that Dr. Liam Argent had the rockstar look down. His hair—the color a mix of dark brown and sun-kissed gold—fell across his forehead in artful disarray. Her gaze moved to his square jaw, coated in dark stubble, and back up to his high cheekbones that were gaining color by the second. His glasses were heavy black frames that'd look ridiculous on anyone else, but on him they only magnified the intensity of his eyes, the color somewhere between liquid silver and matte gray, depending on his mood.

He'd worn his customary white lab coat, khaki pants, and boots. Ordinary dorky-scientist garb. But the colorful tattoos visible beneath the collar of his lab coat, tattoos that started on his right hand and traveled up his wrist, were anything but ordinary. She'd never gotten more than a glimpse of his tats, since they were sworn enemies and all.

He loomed over her, his lips pulled into a flat line. "What is this about, Miss Gradsky?"

Stirling smiled at him and reached out to straighten his pocket protector. How nerdy that he always wore this ugly plastic thing jammed with stuff. "The Weed Worshipers wanted to personally thank you for your scientific contributions to building a better bud."

Was it her imagination or did his lips just twitch?

Nah.

"Everyone, this is Dr. Liam Argent. Careful now, he goes Dr. Jekyll when people assume all his job entails is castrating male cannabis plants, deflowering female cannabis plants, and watching them get it on under a microscope."

A few people in the group chuckled.

"As you can see, Miss Gradsky's sense of humor is on par with that of a thirteen-year-old boy."

More laughter.

"Okay, let's show the ball snipper and cherry popper our appreciation. On the count of three. One…two…three…"

"For he's a jolly high fellow, for he's a jolly high fellow, for he's a jolly high fellow… that nobody can deny."

His eyes shot lasers at her. "Thank you. Now if you'll excuse me, I have to get back to work."

Jeff said, "Good luck with your…you know. We'll form a smoke circle in your honor tonight. Keep it up."

The woman next to Jeff elbowed him and hissed, "You don't say 'keep it up' to a sex addict."

"*Former* sex addict," Stirling pointed out with sweet malice.

"The exit is to your left," Dr. Argent said tersely.

After the group filed out, Dr. Mad Scientist got in her face. "What part of 'no visitors in the lab' is unclear to you?"

"Oh, that lame-ass rule was totally negated when *you* dug up the Weed Worshipers and awarded them 'an exclusive, all-access tour of cannabis Mecca' given by me—the one true believer in becoming an 'elevationist' in the cannabis church movement."

"I have no idea what you're talking about."

"Like you had *no idea* how the air horn got duct taped to the bottom of my office chair?" she demanded.

He cocked his head. "I've told you to discuss it with the cleaning service. Didn't you recommend that I talk to them after I discovered Kentucky blue grass growing in my spare keyboard?"

She tsk-tsked. "So few people have job pride anymore." She poked him in the chest. "You should consider yourself lucky that I didn't demand you do something 'science-y' for the Weed Worshipers."

"*Science-y* isn't even a word, Miss Gradsky. At any rate, I'm not subject to your whims."

"You couldn't satisfy my whims even if I deigned to let you try."

"I believe you're equating the term 'whim' with the word 'fantasy.' But I'll admit I have imagined you wearing a ball gag during meetings."

"Aha! Then you also admit clipping that 'Why Men Prefer Submissive Women' article to my monitor with a dog leash and collar." She'd actually had to close her door, she'd started laughing so hard when she'd seen that one.

He blinked at her. "I would never violate the sanctity of your sacred space. Not that *you* adhere to the same respect for privacy. Was it really necessary to include a case of 'Self-love Lube' with my lab supplies?"

"Since I have no clue what you're doing in your secret lab, Dexter—"

"I can assure you that I'm not jacking off all goddamn day."

They stared at each other, neither one backing down.

"And what was the nonsense about me being a sex addict?" he demanded.

"Ask the blow-up doll in your office." Stirling opened the door and said, "Peace out, yo," tacking on "Dr. Dickhead," under her breath as she escaped.

Chapter Two

Dr. Dickhead.

Liam watched that round butt of hers sway as she walked off.

He'd tried—God, how he'd tried—to ignore her taunts, but Stirling Gradsky challenged him at every turn. The woman was a menace. A smart menace, a sexy menace, but still a nuisance and a distraction nonetheless.

When he'd signed on to be the director of research at High Society, he'd anticipated a fresh start. No workplace drama like he'd dealt with at his former position in California. But he'd had a run-in with Stirling on the very first day.

She'd informed him that he was required to turn in his research notes at the end of every week so she could go over them.

Liam balked at that. Not only were his notes in shorthand only he could decipher, but he doubted Miss Dreadlocks and Multiple Piercings had the educational background to understand complex biology—and then Liam said as much to her.

Wrong thing to say.

Evidently Stirling had a master's degree in biology.

And how did he respond to that? Tell her that he was excited to work with someone he wouldn't have to explain things to fifteen times?

No. He'd said, "Well, it's not quite on par with my *doctorate* in microbiology from MIT, is it?"

Stirling wasn't the only one shocked by his reply. Liam cringed even now when he remembered what a condescending dick he'd been.

So their working relationship had started out antagonistically.

Every time he opened his mouth to speak to her, some alien took control of his brain.

He'd earned the Dr. Dickhead name. As well as Arrogant Asshole. One time he'd overheard her call him Liam the Lab Loser... That one stung. He'd lived with that attitude from his sophomore year in high school until he'd graduated from college. So what if he preferred to be in the lab, studying micro-organisms and deciphering covalent bonds. That was a more productive use of his time than bonding with juvenile frat boys. He'd gone to college to learn, not to party, not to hook up with a different girl every weekend—not that that had ever been an issue. Hot co-eds didn't hang around in the lab, and even if they had, a geek like him wasn't on their radar.

By the time he'd earned his doctorate, he'd gained confidence, not only in his work but in himself. He'd achieved every goal he'd set for himself in that tiny two-bedroom apartment he'd shared with Gramma. She'd lived to see him graduate from college, but she'd passed on the next year. Liam still missed her. When things went to hell in California, his first thought was: *I want to go home.*

And here he was. Back in Denver. With a great job, a killer apartment, money in the bank...and the high point of every workday the last ten months was when he and Stirling crossed paths. The zany woman had executed some killer pranks. He'd had a hard time staying aloof—but that was part of their game.

Last week she'd double-pranked him. The fake message with the crude name had been funny on its own. But she'd padlocked his lunch box. When he'd finally picked the lock, he'd discovered she'd replaced his lunch with vagina-shaped suckers.

Classic.

He removed his glasses and set them on the countertop. His vision had gone blurry from staring through a microscope all day. He rubbed his eyes—as if that would help—and scrubbed his palms on his face. In the last few days his stubble had grown to that itchy stage. No matter how late he left tonight, he had to stop at the store and buy some razors.

As he contemplated packing it in early for once, his cell phone buzzed. He fished it out of the front pocket of his lab coat and squinted at the caller ID: MACON GRADSKY. He poked the *answer call* icon. "Hello, Macon. What's up?"

"Not my stocks, that's for damn sure."

Liam chuckled. "I doubt that. You're too savvy to be on the

downward slide for long. And I'm too savvy to know you didn't call me to shoot the shit."

"One of these days I'll shock the hell out of you and do just that. I may even give you one of those bro hugs."

"Dude. Anything but that. So what's going on?"

He paused. "It occurred to me we haven't had an official meeting this month. I've been putting out other fires and need to catch up as to where we are. So clear the conference room of objects that could be used as weapons, because Stirling will be at the meeting."

"Great. Looking forward to it."

Macon snorted. "You can't lie for shit, Argent."

He did smile at that.

"I have an idea. Bring some product samples to the meeting. You and my sister both need to mellow out."

Liam slipped his phone back in his pocket and shoved his glasses on his face. So much for his plan to skip out early.

* * * *

Stirling was already in the conference room when Liam strolled in.

Naturallly she'd selected the seat at the head of the table.

She glanced up at him. For just a moment, she looked at him without pretense.

He liked seeing her without her defenses up. So he smiled at her. "Hey."

Her pale blue eyes narrowed.

And…they were back to being adversaries—not even friendly adversaries—where they'd been stuck for the entirety of the time they'd known each other.

The time had come to change that.

Stirling's gaze zoomed to the binder tucked under his arm. "Is that Dr. Argent's precious notebook that no one has been allowed to access because we don't possess the intellectual ability to crack your super-secret code?"

Liam set the binder on his end of the table and pushed it so it slid across the table to her end. "Have at it."

"Knock off the fake I'm-a-team-player attitude. My brother won't believe it any more than I do."

He slammed his hands down on the table and she jumped.

"Enough. We're not enemies, Miss Gradsky. We are coworkers. It's exhausting to constantly look over my shoulder to see what form of torture you'll inflict on me next. So, please. Can we call a truce?"

"For real?"

He raised his left eyebrow. "You prefer a blood oath? Fine. You first."

She laughed. A real laugh—not that evil chuckle he was used to hearing from her.

And the smile that accompanied her laugh? Beautiful.

"I deserved that." She smiled again. "Truce."

"Thank God." Liam dropped into the chair opposite her end of the table.

Stirling drummed her fingernails on the top of the binder. She studied him with curiosity, not hostility. "Are these really your notes?"

"Some of them. The rest are in my office."

"For the past ten months you've led me on a merry chase regarding your research."

He shrugged. "I didn't trust you after you subjected me to the stripper 'lab assistant'"—he made air quotes—"who had her breasts in my face so I couldn't even look in my microscope without getting an eyeful of her cleavage. Then I caught her pawing through my desk right after she'd tried to stick her hand down my pants."

"Misty wasn't a stripper."

He leaned forward. "Seriously, Stirling? You're trying to convince me that *Misty Rain* wasn't a stripper?"

"Fine. She was a stripper. And a high-priced one." She sighed. "I can't believe that didn't work."

"So that's why you considered sending a half-naked gay cowboy into my lab? To see if I preferred…man meat over a taco?"

Stirling choked on her water. Then she started laughing so hard that it took several long moments for her to stop. "Man meat? Taco?"

"I wasn't sure if using the words cock and pussy would offend your delicate sensibilities."

"Jesus, Liam, you're funny."

That was the first time she'd used his name without attaching some snarky insult to it. He folded his arms over his chest. "Did you ever consider if you just asked me nicely, and acted as if you sincerely cared about what I'd been working on, that I would've given you access to my research notes?"

That startled her. Then she groaned. "All I would've had to do was say *please?*"

"Or bribed me with an ounce of premium weed—specifically the Girl Scout Cookies strain. That's my go-to smoke when I've had a shit day."

Stirling's blue eyes lit up. "Really? Mine too." A pause. "Wait. Now I remember. The late meeting. Like three months ago. You were in a bad mood."

"I'm surprised you remember, given you probably believe I'm always in a bad mood."

"Truce much, asswipe?" she retorted.

He sighed. "Sorry. That day in particular I ended up in a bad headspace." His ex had called, trying to grill him about what he was working on. Making promises about all the perks he'd get—including her—if he came back to work at GreenTech. When he'd laughed, she showed him her nasty, cutthroat side and a reminder of why he'd left.

"You perked right up when I whipped out the new vaporizer pen and loaded it with the chocolaty, minty goodness of the Girl Scout Cookies variety of cannabis buds."

He remembered the first hit of that sweet smoke. "So those buds were from your personal stash?"

"Yeah. And I don't share my weed with just anyone. But you really needed something to level you out. I'd never seen you that unhappy. So I was glad to help you, even if it was just in a small way." She seemed surprised she'd admitted that.

Liam realized that was Stirling offering an olive branch. "It was not a small thing and I'm grateful for your generosity. Maybe I can return the favor and we can smoke together again, this time from my personal stash."

"I'd like that."

They stared at one another, a different sort of awareness stretching between them.

Stirling patted the book. "You don't mind if I flip through this as we're waiting for Macon?"

"Knock yourself out." He smirked. "Figuratively speaking, of course."

"Of course."

While she pored over the pages, Liam snagged a sparkling water from the mini fridge.

Stirling squinted at the corner of one page, lifting the binder up and tilting it to achieve a better angle. Then a sneaky smile curled her lips and she looked absolutely adorable.

Of all the adjectives you could assign to her, you choose...adorable? Not hot-as-fuck?

"Dude. Did you really draw an effigy of me?"

"Yes."

"When?"

He refused to be embarrassed. "During the full staff meeting where you forced everyone to participate in 'trust building' exercises."

Amused, she said, "Not fond of corporate bonding techniques?"

"I've never understood the purpose of them. It's a waste of time."

"It's a waste of my time if you're doodling during the meeting," she pointed out.

That's when he felt slightly guilty. "I apologize. But it is a pretty good likeness, isn't it?"

"Your rendering of my dreads is quite good. Yet I'm surprised you didn't fashion them into snakes to cement my similarity to Medusa."

"You sound disappointed."

"I'm not. It's just..." She tilted her head, sending those white-blond dreads tumbling over her shoulder like bleached-out ropes. "I would've drawn devil horns on you. Maybe blackened out a couple of teeth. Given you a beaver's tail and a peg leg."

He reached into his pocket protector, withdrew a mechanical pencil, and rolled it across the table to her. "Prove it."

"You're joking."

"You know you want to even the score."

"What makes you think I can draw?"

Liam lifted an eyebrow. "I'm supposed to believe that someone *else* at High Society drew a sack and four penises on the back window of my car with the phrase 'Eat a bag of dicks, asshat'?"

She opened her mouth to deny it when Macon hustled into the room.

He wore a Western-cut suit, cowboy boots, and a black hat. The suit wasn't stylish; it veered close to cheap looking and tacky. Macon knew he came across as a hick ambulance-chasing lawyer, but that served him well. This persona was just that—a skin he slipped on when it suited him and slithered out of when he accomplished his goal. His adversaries in court wouldn't recognize him outside the courtroom—

which was exactly why he dressed as he did.

"There's no blood on the walls, floor, or conference table, so I'm assuming one of you just got here?" Macon said to Stirling.

"Actually, Dr. Argent and I are taking a stab at civility."

Liam fought a smile. "Apt choice of phrasing, Miss Gradsky. But I concur."

Macon rolled his eyes. "Jesus. This is the one place I come to get away from lawyer speak, so knock that formal vocab shit off right now. And move down to this end of the table. This isn't *Game of Thrones.*"

When Liam said, "The iron throne is mine," Stirling said the same thing.

Their eyes caught and they both laughed.

"I feel like I've stepped into an alternate dimension."

Liam muttered, "You're not the only one," as he walked over to claim the seat next to Stirling.

Macon popped the locks on his beat-up briefcase. "Speaking of..." He pulled out a top of the line vaporizer pen and clicked it five times to ignite it.

"Bad day?" Stirling asked.

"You have no idea. TGIF." He brought the pen to his mouth and inhaled.

"Umm... It's Thursday, not Friday, bro."

Liam gave Stirling a sideways glance. She seemed nonplussed about her brother's behavior.

"So? Why'd you call a meeting when it appears you're ready to get your buzz on?"

He exhaled. "Not a buzz, little sis. This is a *boost* because my workday won't end until midnight."

Stirling said, "Your boss is a hardass," fully aware that Macon ran his own law firm.

"And I've heard he's a smartass too," Liam added.

Ignoring their jabs, Macon rested his elbows on the conference table and addressed Stirling. "The recreational store had a dip in revenue last month. What happened?"

Stirling jutted out that stubborn jaw, and Liam found it hard to concentrate on her words and not how perfectly plush her lips were. "We were out of stock on just about every edible we carry. We sold the fresh cookies and bars from Wake and Bake the same day they delivered them. And they can't keep up with demand on their end, so increasing our order isn't an option. The gummies, suckers, mints—all the prepackaged edibles—the suppliers ran out, again due to higher than expected demand across the city. Nothing we can do about that. Oh right, except buy that industrial-size supercritical CO_2 extraction machine, so even if we opt not to create and sell our own edibles, we can resell the refined products—whether it's oil, wax, or resin, since evidently there's a shortage."

Liam nodded.

"You're the one who keeps telling me we don't need to expand," Macon said.

"We don't. This machine would be added *value*, not expansion."

"Revenue is down. And that machine and the vacuum ovens are astronomically expensive."

"Is it less expensive than the equipment you purchased for Dr. Argent's secret lab? Has *that* paid off?"

Macon glanced at Liam. "Last time we spoke you'd successfully spliced two heirloom strains. Where are you on that?"

"Splicing only produced me four live plants to work with, and two of those were culled for pollination in case I do get positive results. They're in second stage grow right now."

"Any indication whether the new strain will have a higher yield?"

Liam bristled. "I'll remind you that I didn't sign on to increase the size of your recreational cash crop."

Silence.

Then Macon said, "I'd hoped that higher yield would be a positive side effect of your experimentation."

"Hoped?" Stirling repeated.

Liam deflected the conversation. "You have Artie managing the grow. He's rotating twenty-four cannabis varieties. Most commercial growers with a retail store aren't offering their clientele half that many premium options. It's not like we're cannibalizing the recreational side to support my work on the medical side."

"So what exactly is it that you *do* around here if Artie is managing the grow?" she asked.

But Macon talked over her and the question was lost. "You developed a medical strain that met with great success, which is why I hired you."

No, you hired me because you want to win the 420 Cup.

"Whoa." Stirling made a time-out sign. "You both lost me. Back up.

Explain Dr. Argent's success with developing a new medical strain."

That was humbling. Stirling didn't know anything about his prior accomplishment. But then again, few people did since he'd signed nondisclosures. Still, it made no sense that Macon hadn't told his business partner about his qualifications.

This was not good. So much for their truce.

"If you two weren't so goddamned busy fighting maybe you would've had a normal conversation between colleagues. So I'll spell it out for you, sis." Macon pointed at Liam. "Ever heard of the Livin' Large variety?"

"Of course I have," she snapped. "It's the premier CBN strain owned by a Dutch pharmaceutical company. It's had excellent results alleviating several common ailments cancer patients suffer from during and after chemotherapy. What does that have to do with this?"

"Everything. Dr. Liam Argent bred that hybrid strain. Think about it. The varietal name is pretty fucking clever."

A beat passed. "*L* from his first name and *arge* from his last name," she muttered and blew out a breath. "Fine. So you're some kind of ganja rockstar god for your cannabis creation. But that just makes me even more suspicious of why'd you'd come to work for us. We're nobody. We're not large scale. Hell, we're not even medium scale."

"I came to work here because I grew up in Denver and I was tired of California."

"That's it?" she demanded.

"No. My previous employer fucked me over. The Dutch company paid GreenTech, the research facility I worked in, millions for the right to register the name with the international plant registry. I was allowed to name the strain but not tell anyone I'd created it. That right belonged to GreenTech." He felt like an idiot admitting that he'd signed away his ownership rights in his employment contract. "I wanted to continue the work I'd been doing and Macon promised me minimal oversight." And a one-year contract. Somehow he didn't think Stirling knew about that, either.

"That's why you refused to show me what you were working on. Afraid I was going to steal it?"

Liam felt her glare—as hot as a Bunsen burner—and met it head on. "Like I mentioned earlier, had you just *asked* me nicely, Miss Gradsky, I would've been happy to accommodate you. But it doesn't change the truth that anyone with a handful of cannabis seeds, a place to grow, and access to the Internet can cultivate and clone cannabis. And yes, I'm completely aware that the goal in a commercial facility is growing bigger buds, which equals higher yields and more money. But it'd be a waste of the top of the line scientific instruments in my lab, and a waste of my doctorate in microbiology, to be quite frank, to focus my expertise solely on increasing quantity."

Throw Macon under the bus? Or let the bus plow over him?

No brainer.

Brace yourself, Macon.

"Besides, Macon was aware I'd be focused on continuing my work isolating CBD and CBN characteristics to build phytocannabinoid profiles and further break down each pharmacological effect."

Macon opened his mouth to comment, but Stirling shut him down. "You hired him to do research that we don't need? And doesn't add any value to our business?"

Ouch. Seemed the bus had hit him as well.

"Yes, Liam is a scientist with loftier and nobler goals than peddling premium pot." Macon shot him a look. "Giving him autonomy and not filling you in on his role here was an error in judgment on my part."

"You're damn right it was. We're supposed to be *partners*. You know that I sank every cent I had into this venture. I trusted your judgment across the board. I didn't even question your initial projected numbers for ROI." She paused and glared at Macon. "How inflated were they?"

"Only by two percent. And stretched out over forty-eight months instead of twenty-four months."

Stirling stood and slapped her hands on the table in front of her brother. "And you have the balls to bring up *one month's* lower than expected revenue with me? When it appears I'll have to wait four fucking years to earn back what I put in?"

Macon said, "The bottom line is we need to expand."

"Bigger is *not* better. I don't know how many times I have to tell you that. You know that is not what I wanted."

"No, *you* didn't want to deal with the plant side from the start, so I hired Dr. Argent to do that. You insisted on setting up the rec store. Dealing with vendors. Choosing the right budtenders. Hiring other knowledgeable employees, a website guru, a graphic designer for branding and ads. You put it all together so the space had a good *vibe*."

"I never intended for my contribution to this business to be managing employees and ordering stock. There's far more to running the front end that I'm not getting to do because I'm stuck working fourteen plus hours every day."

"I guess we're both wrong in our expectations, aren't we?"

Stirling made a growling noise that set the hair on the back of Liam's neck on end.

Macon sighed. "I admit I haven't been focused on this business, with running my law practice—"

"Save it. I'm done." She stormed toward the exit, her dreadlocks swaying across her back.

"Done? What do you mean done?" Macon demanded.

Stirling didn't even turn around as she flipped him off and slammed the door behind her.

And things had been going so well.

For about twenty minutes.

Macon tossed his vape pen in his briefcase and snapped the locks. He pushed to his feet.

"Where do you think you're going?" Liam asked.

"To smooth things over with my sister."

"Leave her be."

"Right. It'll be ten times worse if—"

"You track her down and come up with more bullshit excuses?" he said tightly.

Macon hung his head.

"Why not just tell her that you hired me to craft a new strain to enter into the 420 Cup while I was working on research?"

"Because neither of those things matter to her. The 420 Cup was created to showcase new cannabis businesses, which is why we can only enter it one time. Wacky Tobaccky built their multimillion-dollar business on winning it. So did Green Machine—and they're the two largest volume dispensaries in Colorado. The impact of winning the cup will wear off, but not in its third year. You knocked it out of the park with our entry, Liam. That is the smoothest indica-sativa hybrid I've ever smoked. Winning that award would be a game changer on so many levels for High Society, and we both know it."

"Again, not to sound like a broken record, but why not just tell Stirling that?"

"Because she's already overworked and she'll just see more recognition as more work. My former Big Ag, corporate executive sister is a pot purist. She argues that we'll continue to set ourselves apart by providing customers with a personalized boutique experience, and not becoming the Costco of cannabis." He snorted. "Putting the business in beer terms—I'm Coors and she's a craft brewery."

"Partners usually have a singular vision. You've been alternately micromanaging petty matters and ignoring major points of contention." Liam narrowed his eyes. "Did you intentionally pit me against Stirling? Ensuring we each kept our own agendas instead of developing a common goal?"

"Oh, hell no. I'll shoulder the blame for my shortsightedness in the name of profit and following my gut instead of a preset financial strategy, but I had nothing to do with you and Stirling butting heads from day one."

"Fair enough." But Macon couldn't deny that he'd kept the grow and the retail side as separate entities. With limited staff, Liam and Stirling had been too busy in their respective departments to get to know each other, to say nothing of really working together. "Have you heard when they're announcing the 420 Cup winner?"

"I'm expecting the call—win or lose—any day."

If they didn't win, would Macon let him go when the one-year contract was up? Liam had forced himself not to think about it.

"Look, will you tell Stirling we'll reconvene same time tomorrow? I'll figure something out between now and then."

Liam pointed at him. "There's your problem. You and *Stirling* need to figure it out."

"And we will. Tomorrow." Macon's cell phone rang and he answered it as he sailed out the door.

After picking up his binder, Liam headed for Stirling's office.

He knocked and waited.

No response.

At least he hadn't heard her cocking a pistol or racking a shotgun.

Liam knocked again. "Stirling. It's Liam. Macon left."

Silence.

He turned the handle and found the door unlocked. As he slowly pushed it open, he thought, *Please don't let the door be booby-trapped.*

He'd pulled that prank on her after she'd put powdered Kool-Aid in his lab gloves, turning his hands vivid purple. A man could only stand so many "Did you jack off Barney?" jokes before he snapped. He added color to Stirling's life by placing a plastic bucket filled with red Jell-O mix and powdery fine glitter above the door. The next morning he'd literally caught her red-faced and red-handed.

Liam eased the door open and said, "Stirling? I'm coming in."

She stood in front of the windows with her back to him.

"Are you okay?"

"No. Did my brother send you?"

"No. I stopped him from storming in here and making things worse."

"I don't know how they could get any worse."

His gut tightened at her clipped tone. Without thinking, he moved in behind her and rested his hands on her shoulders, just wanting to...soothe her.

And it was very telling, how lost she was in her own head that she didn't flinch or shrug him off.

"Talk to me," he said softly.

"About what?"

"About everything."

"I don't even know where to start."

"How about at the beginning? Where we should've started months ago."

Stirling tensed up. "I can't."

"Why not?"

"I'm too goddamned mad to think straight right now."

He grinned. In the reflection of the window he saw her stick her tongue out at him. "Lucky for you, Miss Gradsky, I have the perfect outlet for that anger."

She started to argue, but he cut her off.

"Before you assume that my suggestion is sexual in nature, I'll add that my anger management solution involves boxing gloves and a heavy bag."

Stirling faced him. "Are you serious? Because I could totally beat the shit out of something right now."

"I have a full kick boxing setup at my place."

Her eyes searched his. "So you're what...inviting me over?"

"Yes." His pulse kicked up a notch or thirty. "We need to talk. You need to punch the fuck out of my heavy bag. While you're doing that and getting your head together, I'll cook dinner for us."

"You cook?"

Liam snagged one of her dreadlocks and tugged it. "Throwing pasta in a pan is much easier than gene splicing."

"True."

"Even if you don't trust my culinary skills, Stirling, don't deny that after that shitshow of a meeting with Macon, we're long overdue for a serious discussion."

"I don't deny it."

"Good. I'll text you my address." He took a couple of steps back. "Don't overthink this and convince yourself not to show up."

No surprise that guilt flashed in her eyes.

"Punching, pasta, and conversation." Liam smiled at her. "That's it."

"Okay. But attempt any funny business, Dr. Pushy, and I'm punching you with your own gloves."

Chapter Three

Stirling's mood didn't change during the thirty minutes it took her to lock up and drive over to Liam's house. She double checked the number on the front of the brick duplex against the text message and parked in the empty space on the street.

Backpack in hand, she jogged up the sidewalk. She'd held her rage, disillusionment, and self-recriminations at bay until that moment when she could let her fists fly.

A set of wide stone steps led to a small porch, surrounded on three sides by a wrought-iron railing. An enormous lilac bush separated the duplex's entrances, offering additional privacy. In this older section of Denver, the well-established vines climbed the bricks and twisted around the fence. This house looked exactly like the kind of place that a stuffy professor—or a tight-ass scientist—would call home.

None of that. A truce means no name calling, no matter how funny some of the names are.

She poked the doorbell.

Immediately the curved wooden door opened, almost as if he'd been standing there, anxious for her arrival.

"Hey."

"Hey." Her fingers tightened on the strap of her backpack as she followed him into the foyer.

Liam pointed up the stairs. "The workout room is the first door on your left. There's a variety of gloves and hand wraps. Feel free to hook your phone up to the stereo system and play music as loud as you want. My neighbor is hard of hearing and this old house is solidly soundproofed."

"Even against screams?" she blurted out.

Those silver-hued eyes of his softened and he reached out as if to reassure her.

She'd start bawling if he showed her kindness. Right now she needed to give her anger an outlet. Civility would have to wait. "Uh, thanks."

"Take as much time as you need. Come find me in the kitchen when you're done."

* * * *

Everything blurred together—the repetitive thud of her gloves, the speed metal blasting from her phone, the creak of the chain holding the heavy bag, and her harsh grunts breaking free with each hard punch. Uncertainty, and anger drove her until exhaustion had her clinging to the heavy bag. She inhaled. Exhaled. Letting her tears fall down her face to mix with the sweat dripping from her chin. She needed to get it all out of her system now, break down in solitude.

Once she'd regained control, she collected herself as she mopped her face with a hand towel. What was that old adage? Never let them see you sweat?

Wrong. Better to show them sweat and blood than tears.

Stirling returned downstairs, confident in her ability to be rational and remain cool-headed and professional.

Holy shit.

She froze in the open doorway to the kitchen.

How in the hell was she supposed to remain professional when she finally got to see Dr. Liam Argent without his trusty lab coat?

Talk about giving "tight ass" a whole new meaning. Had his jeans been custom made to perfectly mold that bitable backside?

Her gaze moved up, skimming across his wide shoulders. The dark gray T-shirt was contoured in all the right places, showcasing his impressive biceps. His tattoo started at the knuckles of his right hand, continuing up the front and back of his forearm until the colorful ink disappeared beneath the sleeve of his T-shirt.

Just how much of his surprisingly buff body was inked?

Liam chose that moment to turn around. Unlike her, his gaze didn't leave her face. "Better?"

"Much. Thank you. I'll warn ya... I probably reek since I don't have a change of clothes."

He shrugged. "After dealing with terpenes all day, nothing bothers me."

"I had no clue what terpenes were until a guy in my freshman year took me to his place and turned me loose in his grow house. I'll never forget how surprising it was to pick out those individual aromas—terpenes—when I rubbed on different plants' leaves. I always thought pot was pot and all marijuana plants smelled the same. Even now that I'm educated on the scent of different terpenes, I don't understand how smokers seek out weed with that cheesy funk smell. My gag reflex kicks in. I prefer varieties with a floral, fuel, fruit, or pine aroma."

"Hence why terpenes are so important and why we need to educate consumers on the impact their cannabis choice will have on them. What smells good to you will taste good when you smoke. Scientifically speaking, all the cannabis compounds interact synergistically to create an 'entourage effect' that magnifies the therapeutic benefits of the plant's individual components—so we can see that the medicinal impact of the whole plant is greater than the sum of its parts. That is what fascinates me."

Stirling blinked at him.

He groaned. "I apologize in advance for slipping into lecture mode. I drift into that when I'm passionate about something and I tend to go into excessive detail...or so I've been told." He blushed. "Not that you need me to explain things to you, since you have a scientific background."

The man was so damn cute when he was flustered.

"Put me out of my misery, please, and let's eat." He pointed to an alcove which held a round table and four chairs. "Dinner is done."

He'd laid out two place settings. She sat near the counter and checked out his living room. A gray, black, and red plaid couch, a black leather recliner, a metal coffee table, and a gray wingback chair were arranged on a vivid scarlet rug. Art decorated the walls. Impressive and not at all what she'd expected.

Liam slid a plate in front of her. "Linguine with pesto and parmesan."

"Looks and smells delicious."

"Thanks. It's my go-to dish when I want a fast meal."

They ate in relative silence.

Stirling snuck looks at Liam, wondering what caused his brow to furrow behind his glasses. She probably should've been organizing her thoughts for their impending conversation, but she couldn't stop her eyes from tracking over his ropy forearms, his broad shoulders, and the muscular definition in his chest. Seeing him in street clothes reiterated the fact that Dr. Liam Argent was hot as fire.

"Stirling? You okay? You look flushed."

Busted. "Lingering effect from my heavy bag session."

"I'll get you a glass of water." He picked up both of their empty plates and retreated to the kitchen.

Who was this solicitous hunk? What happened to Dr. Condescending, Calculating, and Contrary?

He froze next to the table when he caught her eyeballing him. "What?"

"It's really strange that we're basically strangers and we've worked together for ten months."

He relaxed. "I agree."

"I'm not being sarcastic when I ask... How do we do this? Drop the shields and the preconceived ideas we've had about each other and really get to know each other?"

"We talk about our life's triumphs and failures." Liam's grin was nothing short of dazzling. "But I say we get high first."

"Omigod, I knew it! You invited me to your place to get me stoned out of my mind so I'd have sex with you."

His smile died and his cheeks flushed.

The man was adorable and delectable. She was totally fucked.

"Umm, actually—"

"I was just giving you shit, Dr. Strangelove. That's what friends do."

"Just for that, Miss Gradsky, I'm making you go first." He set down her glass of water. "And I'm not talking about who gets the first hit."

Smiling, she followed him into the living room.

He perched on the edge of the couch and pulled out a plain wooden box from the lower shelf of the coffee table. As soon as he opened the lid, the sweet, pungent scent of cannabis drifted out.

"So what variety is our dessert?"

"Guess." He popped the top of the small glass container right under her nose.

She sniffed. "Definitely fuel based. Slight hint of lemon on the back end. I'm guessing...Sour D?"

Liam smiled at her. "Close. Sour Amnesia. The back end of this one is a skunky spice, not citrus. This one is more uplifting than brain fogging." He bumped his shoulder into hers. "Good nose. Maybe you *should* keep running the retail store."

"Piss off."

He laughed.

She tried not to react to that sexy, husky deep laugh.

And she really tried not to notice how dexterous his long fingers were as he prepped the pipe. But every motion seemed overtly sexual. How lovingly he stroked the glass. How firmly his thumb pressed into the flint on the lighter as he adjusted the level of the flame. How reverently he broke up the bud and then lifted his fingers to his nose, closing his eyes as he inhaled that unique fragrance.

Stirling imagined those long fingers of his sliding down between her legs. Teasing. Stroking. Fingering her with the same adept touch. Then bringing proof of her arousal between them. Holding his damp fingers coated in her essence, right there for her to see and for him to breathe in. For him to taste.

God yes. Please. It has been so long…

What was wrong with her? She hadn't even taken a hit…and yet she felt that telltale buzz.

"Liam? What kind of herb did you use in your pesto?"

"Basil. Why?"

"Cause I feel…a little fluffy."

"That would be from the cannabis-infused olive oil that I mixed in with the basil."

The man had the audacity to smile at her. Then he brought the pipe to her lips. "Ladies first."

She flicked the lighter, lit the load, and breathed deep into the bottom of her lungs. As she held in the smoke, she passed the pipe to Liam and sank back into the cushions.

Immediately on her exhale a punch of happiness washed over her. She watched him take his turn and then he relaxed into the couch.

After a stretch of silence, Liam said, "You want another hit?"

"Not now. I'm good." She sighed. "Much faster acting than the stuff you snuck into my food."

"Honestly, I grabbed the oil without thinking."

"It wasn't a part of your nefarious plan to seduce me?"

"No."

She heaved an exaggerated sigh. "Well, that's a damn cryin' shame."

"Right." He snorted. "You're definitely high."

"That's the goal."

After a bit, she snickered.

"I *knew* ganja would make you giggly, Gradsky."

"You rock at alliteration."

"I kill at Scrabble too."

"We'll have to play sometime." Stirling turned her head and looked at him. "Wanna hear something funny and ironic?"

"Besides usage in the general populace of the phrase 'soft abrasive'? What advertising genius coined that idiotic axiom? I can guarantee it wasn't a chemist."

She laughed. "You're toasted."

"Like a bagel on Sunday morning. Anyway, continue with funny and ironic."

"I didn't touch weed until I was in grad school."

Liam kept his eyes closed but he quirked his brow. "Why?"

"I had too much ambition and I feared marijuana would dampen that drive."

"A logical observation, but a wrong assumption." He sat up and moved to the corner of the couch, stretching his legs across the cushions. "Do you mind?"

She mimicked his pose on the other end, making room for his long legs. He wasn't wearing socks, and she couldn't help but notice he had sexy feet. Or maybe seeing him so obviously relaxed, barefoot and wearing casual clothes, was what made him so approachably sexy.

"Ah. Thank you. So where were we now that the truth serum is kicking in?"

"I was detailing my sordid past about how trying pot just one time led me to co-owning a marijuana marketplace."

There was that wicked grin of his again. Her stomach did a slow flip. "How did you wind up on the road to ruin, Miss Gradsky?"

"I did my grad work at UC Boulder."

"Enough said."

"Hey now, not nice." She bumped her knee into his. "Anyway, some of the smartest people I studied with were recreational smokers. I figured if it hadn't hurt their brains then I'd try it. Because I was paranoid, I did some research and selected a guy who knew his weed to pop my pot cherry."

Liam frowned.

"He gave me a crash course and I tried different varieties until I found a couple I liked."

"What did you like about it after purposely staying away from it for so long?"

"That I could choose the level of high. It doesn't work that way with booze. And I never felt like crap the next day, unlike doing tequila shots. With booze, I overshot that happy buzz more times than not. I like to be in control."

Those silvery eyes widened behind his glasses. "Really? I hadn't noticed."

She knocked her knee into his again.

"So you became a regular smoker?"

"For a while, when I had a source I trusted in Boulder. After I got the position with GenAgra and moved to Denver, I stopped smoking entirely. Not because of company drug-testing but I was the only woman at that management level and I had it in my head that I needed to set a good example."

After he asked, "How old were you?" he nonchalantly straightened the bottom of her legging and rested his hand on her ankle.

Not a big deal that he's touching you. Keep talking. "I finished my undergrad degree in three years so I was twenty-three when I graduated from UC with my masters. I considered myself lucky to get that job."

"I'll bet you did, with the dreads and the piercings."

She blinked at him. "Oh, God no. Back then I looked like I'd walked straight out of the 'how to dress for corporate success' handbook. Sleek blond bob, business suits—not too tight—in neutral colors. My blouses were feminine—but not low-cut—because heaven forbid my cleavage would ever show."

His gaze slid down to her chest and lingered. "Good riddance to the Amish work wear."

Heat bloomed on her cheeks. "So for the next five years I worked a minimum of sixty-hours a week. I made myself indispensable—or so I believed."

"I'm familiar with that mindset."

"A few things pushed me into questioning my quality of life. My sister London had a baby. I had to cancel a vacation I'd booked a year in advance because of some crisis at work, which turned out to be nothing but the big boss passing the buck until it hit me. I was a frazzled, angry mess and I needed to find a way to de-stress. About that time medicinal cannabis dispensaries started popping up all over Denver. On a whim I ducked into one far away from my work and my apartment."

He chuckled. "I'm imagining you skulking around, wearing a trench coat and a fedora, trying to be inconspicuous."

"Ha ha. No. I dressed in a lab coat and bullied my way in like a know-it-all scientist."

He pinched her. "Not nice."

"I got my diagnosis and my prescription."

"Did your…prescription affect your job performance?"

She shrugged. "No. Except maybe I had more clarity."

"About?"

"My life. Myself. My role in the company. I couldn't deny my disillusionment. I'd been unable to implement the ideas I'd brought as that gung-ho grad student. I'd started to wonder if they hired me to fill a quota. I began to see and hear the sexism, and once you're aware of it, you can't be unaware again. It'd spilled from my work life into my personal life and I hadn't realized it."

His gaze turned sharp. "Details."

"At the time I had a boyfriend, Nick, who worked for the same company but in a different department. He was one of those good-looking, smooth-talking sales guys. The type of man who never looked twice at a woman like me. So when he lavished attention on me…"

"You fell for it."

"Hook, line, and sinker. My higher position meant I earned more money than he did. He claimed it wasn't an issue and I believed him, even when he expected me to pay for things since my paycheck eclipsed his. Outside of work, I took on the traditional role of cook and housekeeper. His role was appreciating all I did for him as he parked his ass in front of the TV."

"Sounds like a real prince."

"Did you say a real prick?" She sneered. "Why yes, he was."

"I'm sure Nick the Prick didn't understand your need to de-stress."

"No. And he was very condescending about my *juvenile excuse to be a pothead*. But drinking bourbon three or four nights a week until you pass out is *so* much more mature."

"Same old argument we're hearing even now, when cannabis is a legal, adult choice," he grumbled. "But go on."

"For the last year Nick and I were a couple, my male bosses kept asking when 'Nick was gonna make an honest woman of me.' I laughed it off—good-old-boy, old-school attitude I'd learned to deal with, right? Then it all came crashing down at a company cocktail party. Booze was flowing, lips were loose. I spent the majority of the evening dealing with a supplier issue so the big bosses could get hammered on free top-shelf liquor and brag about the size of their bank accounts and their dicks. Somehow I ended up overhearing my direct supervisor and my boyfriend discussing my future. Nick practically guaranteed that after we were married and he knocked me up I'd become a stay-at-home mom. That betrayal was bad enough. But when my supervisor said he'd have me start training Nick to take over my position? I had a reality check."

Liam swept his thumb across her ankle bone, creating a tingle of awareness that zipped all the way up to the nape of her neck. "I hope you beat the fuck out of Nick the Prick right there, in front of all your big bosses, so they saw firsthand what a loser pussy he was."

"I hadn't grown a pair of balls yet." She paused to catch her breath. "You know...have you ever really thought about that phrase? How derogatory it is? Like women are inferior because we don't have a hairy nut sac? Like that wrinkly, dangling thing between a man's legs is a source of power? And we somehow need a pair of them to be strong?" Her indignation grew. "As of right now I'm banning that phrase. Women don't need to grow balls to be tough. We grow human beings. *Inside* our bodies. So from this point on, when a dude pisses me off? I'm gonna tell him to woman up and grow a goddamn uterus. Balls are for pussies."

Liam started laughing. His laughter was sexy. And contagious.

Stirling joined in and it was several moments before they regained control.

She was wiping her eyes when Liam said, "You kill me, bulldog. You have since that first day."

"You have an odd way of showing it." She cocked her head. "Bulldog? Is that a nickname?"

"Yes, because you are tenacious."

"But...bulldogs are ugly, mean, and slobbery."

He studied her until she became self-conscious.

"What?"

Then he blushed. "Once again I utterly fail at the nickname game. My last girlfriend always made a kissy face in selfies. So in my need to come up with a term of endearment for her, I called her duck lips."

She gasped. "You did not."

"I did. Just that one time. I never bothered to try out any others." He shook his head. "Stoner segue. Back to you. Finish your story. What happened next after Nick the Prick made his declaration to your boss?"

"I did the typical girly thing and ran home to my mother."

"And?"

"And she listened. She asked the questions I'd been too afraid to ask myself. When I returned to Denver, I broke it off with Nick. I did my job but I didn't put in nearly the hours I had before. So we got behind schedule. When management tried to blame it on me, I pointed out the obvious: I'd been overworked and underpaid for years. I knew they were looking for an excuse to can me. And they found one when we had a random drug test."

He squinted at her. "Is that even legal?"

"Turns out it wasn't. I tested positive for marijuana. When I met with my supervisor, he claimed he'd 'heard' I'd become addicted to pot and my recent poor performance proved it."

"I presume Nick the Prick brought his concerns about you to his new buddy, your boss?"

She nodded. Thinking about that now, even a few years later, still brought a lump to her throat. Nick, that rat bastard, a man she thought she'd loved…had betrayed her. "I suffered through my supervisor's lecture on GenAgra's 'family values' philosophy, which he followed up with airing his personal disappointment in my 'illegal' activities. Then the bullshit got deeper as he expressed his concern that I'd show up high for client meetings and that would reflect badly on the company. So I was being terminated, effective immediately." She took a breath. "I let him blather, then I let him stew as I sat across from him and said nothing. If the smug look on his face was an indication… he thought he'd cowed me. But he'd forgotten I hadn't reached that level of success by being nice. I pointed out that the department I worked in had issues *before* I took over, and I'd done the workload of my predecessors—which was two men—by myself."

"Did that wipe the smugness away?"

"Yes, especially after I informed him there was nothing illegal about my positive drug test because I *did* have a doctor's prescription for medicinal use of cannabis, so firing me would result in my attorney filing a lawsuit for wrongful termination."

"I'll bet Macon had a field day with that."

"He did. It took a solid year before GenAgra agreed to the

settlement, which was substantial." That reminded her of the blowup with Macon earlier. Sometimes she thought going into business with her brother was the worst decision she'd ever made.

"You and Macon fight, but that's how issues get addressed and resolved. That process works for you." Liam squeezed her foot and moved to sit up. "We both need another hit. Something different this time."

"Any more and I won't be driving home."

He prepped the pipe. "So crash here on the couch. The extra time together will result in us brainstorming a brilliant solution to present to Macon tomorrow."

Stirling spun around and set her feet on the floor. "Us?"

"Why do you think I asked you to come over?"

Talk about a dash of cold water. Had she misread Liam's signals entirely? This...dinner, sharing a smoke, and exchanging life histories was only about improving their working relationship? Why did that bother her so much?

Because you want this to be something different than it's been with him. You've spilled your guts and he's shared nothing.

She said, "What's in it for you?" a little more sharply than she'd intended.

"Less tension in the workplace. It's time I became a team player." He sucked in a huge hit and passed the pipe to her.

For a moment she just held the pipe, wondering if she should set it down, make her excuses, and leave.

After he exhaled, he rested his hand on her thigh. "Stay. Please. This is the best night I've had since I moved to Denver. I like talking to you."

Her heart raced. "Okay. But only if I'm not doing all the talking."

"But I'd much rather listen to you."

"Why?"

Liam handed her the lighter and watched her mouth intently as she lit up and filled her lungs. "It's that husky timbre of your voice. It sounds like..."

She exhaled. "Like I just smoked some premium weed?"

"No. It sounds like sex."

Her vision went hazy and pleasure suffused her entire body.

From the weed? Or from his words?

Through the rush she swore she heard Liam say, "Hot, dirty, sweaty sex. Makes me think that's how you'd sound when your throat was raw from coming so hard, so many times."

This shit was potent if she had hallucinations that Dr. Detached was murmuring in her ear about sex noises.

"What did we just smoke?"

"Something new I've been working on."

"Jesus. We need to sell this. It's fucking amazing."

They sat shoulder to shoulder on the couch, not speaking, but Liam hadn't removed his hand from her leg either.

Don't read anything into it. And for fuck's sake, don't bring it up.

But her brain and her mouth weren't in synch. She found herself saying, "You have big hands."

Grabbing her wrist, he pressed their palms together, holding them up and studying them. "Mine *is* big."

She laughed. "That's what all men say."

His warm lips brushed her ear and he murmured, "Filthy-minded girl."

The left side of her body broke out in goose bumps.

"Just another thing to like about you."

Her mouth had gone bone dry. "I need some water." She shot to her feet, lost her balance, and in trying to right herself, she tweaked her lower back.

"Ow. Fuck, fuck, fuck, fuck!"

Liam scrambled off the couch. "What's wrong?"

Stirling remained bent over at the waist. "I pulled something in my lower back."

"Do you need help straightening up?"

"No!" Oh, wowza. Hanging upside down after the head buzz from that last hit… Not good. Everything was spinning. She slowly dropped her hands to the carpet and then lowered to her knees.

"Is that better?"

She arched her back, trying to pop the muscle into place. The sharp, stabbing pain snapped her resolve to act tough, "Fuck! Fuck, fuck, fuck, fuck, fuck, fuck."

"I'll take that as a no." Liam sank to his knees and peered into her eyes. "What can I do?"

"Rub the spot until whatever is caught snaps back into place." She stretched out, facedown on the floor, and groaned. "But you'll have to take my pants off first."

Chapter Four

Liam's brain got stuck on her husky demand, *Take my pants off.*

Yes, of course. And I prefer to use my teeth.

No.

Not happening. He'd help her work the kinks out—would he *ever* love to help her with that in a completely different context—but if he removed her pants his brain would cease to be of any use to him at all.

She moaned.

"Point to where it hurts," he said.

She reached around and pressed her thumb next to the bone of her right hip. "Here."

Thankfully he only had to slide her pants down to the upper curve of her butt. The lemony scent of her laundry detergent, or her lotion, or maybe that was her skin, teased his nose. As he leaned in closer, he was mad to find the origin of that intoxicating fragrance. Rub his face in it so every time he breathed in he'd be surrounded by her scent.

Take it down a notch, perv.

"Hold still." Replacing her thumb with his fingers, he began to rub the area.

Her body tensed.

He'd never been a "give a woman a massage" type of guy, not even as a precursor to sex. "Tell me if I'm too rough."

"I like it rough. The harder you push into me, the better."

Liam bit back a groan. Christ. She likely hadn't meant it the way he'd taken it, but his brain decided to supply him with images of her naked beneath him anyway, their hands clasped above her head as he drove his cock into her with enough force to rattle the windows.

"Yes. Right there. God, that's the exact spot. More."

Her low whimper started a soundtrack in his head of all the sexy noises he'd wring from her as he meticulously mapped every millimeter of her body with just his mouth.

Don't go there. You're high and horny because this is the first time you've touched a woman since you left California.

He cleared his throat, "Talk to me. Last thing you said was Macon got your settlement a year after he filed suit. What were you doing during that time?"

"Letting out my inner bohemian. Went with the dreads and nose ring." She propped her chin on her forearm and looked over her shoulder at him. "What's the story with your tattoos?"

He muttered, "That's random."

"No, it's your turn to fill in the blanks. Tell me about your tats."

"Is this helping?" He dug his thumb into the flesh between her hip joint and her spine.

"Yes. Keep rubbing. Keep talking. Tats. Stat."

"Why are you so certain there's significance behind them?"

"Because I doubt you do anything without methodically weighing the pros and cons, especially when it comes to something you'll have to live with the rest of your life. And not only do you have a sleeve, the design begins at your knuckles and ends at your neck. That's hardcore ink."

"And I don't seem like a hardcore guy."

"Exactly. Nor do you act like the kind of guy who'd give a damn what anyone thought, one way or the other. Perhaps that's why you did it."

He smiled. "Very astute, Miss Gradsky."

"Thank you, professor. So you might as well tell me because I'm a bulldog when it comes to this stuff."

"Fine. You win." He stopped kneading her back. "Like you mentioned, I'm fully aware of the first impression I make. And you were correct in that I didn't give a damn how others—strangers or colleagues—saw me. I'd started the doctoral program at MIT with the same physical appearance I'd maintained since grad school. Malachi, my assigned partner, was an atypical doctoral candidate. A jai alai player who partied as much as he studied. A leather-jacket-wearing, motorcycle-driving, long-haired gym rat. The utter opposite of me. I suspected I'd be doing ninety percent of our lab work, which suited me fine because I'd be in complete control."

Stirling wiggled her backside. "You stopped rubbing that spot just when it'd started to feel better. Keep going."

"Sorry."

"Keep going with the story, too."

He absentmindedly swept his thumbs over the dimples of her ass as he struggled to multitask. "Malachi changed my life. He challenged me intellectually, socially, physically, emotionally, sexually." He paused. "Not sexually between us, but he refused to let me continue to be a frightened boy when I had the capacity to be a man confident in more than just my intellect."

"I like this Malachi dude already."

Liam smiled. "He would've loved you." And the sly fucker would've tried to seduce Stirling right out from underneath him.

Was he trying to seduce Stirling?

Fuck yeah.

"What happened?"

"I embraced a total life change. I became physically active. I paid attention to my outer appearance. I went to bars and parties. I even talked to girls."

"Uh-oh. Look out, ladies. Liam the Lothario is on the loose, lookin' for lovin'."

He resisted the urge to smack her butt. "Let's just say I had a *lot* of time to make up for and I enjoyed the hell out of every minute of it."

Surprisingly, she had no smart comment for that.

"I didn't feel transformed as much as I discovered the man I'd always wanted to be." *Did that sound hopelessly lame?*

"No, it doesn't sound hopelessly lame."

"I hadn't meant to say that out loud." Goddammit. He hadn't meant to admit that either.

"I'm glad you did. Those cathartic moments are what drive us. So the bad-boy scientist remade you in his image?" she teased.

Sadness executed a one-two punch in his chest. "No. He showed me there's more courage in trying and failing than there is in easy and expected success."

Stirling rolled to her side.

Liam didn't flinch at her intense scrutiny.

"Your tone changed. Something happened to him."

"A freak accident during a jai alai game. The ball hit him in the chest and stopped his heart."

She sat up. "Liam. I'm so sorry."

"I miss that crazy fucker." He offered a sad smile. "He'd be happy that I didn't ease into getting my first tat."

"Wait. You started *out* with an entire sleeve?"

"Two days after I got my doctorate. With the money left over from my grant I booked a group of three tattoo artists and over the course of a week they inked my entire arm."

"So you had the whole design drawn up ahead of time?"

He shook his head. "I told them my interests, influences, and gave them free rein. It was a collaborative effort with no preconceived expectations from me."

"That might be the most daring—and stupid—decision I've ever heard." She accorded him a contemplative look. "Why go so extreme? What was the rush?"

Liam's neck heated. "I was about to start a new job. I didn't want my new coworkers to look at me and assume typical dorky doctor. The tats...felt rebellious, but at the same time, it seemed as if I'd taken another step closer to becoming the best version of myself."

"I get that. So long, Mr. Boring and Buttoned Up. Meet the newly-minted Dr. Tattooed and Tantalizing."

"That's stretching it quite a bit."

"We're running on truth serum, remember? Have you looked at yourself lately?"

When she gestured to him, his gaze zeroed in on the ease of her movement and he changed the subject. "Did the massage help?"

A throaty sigh drifted between them. "You have magic hands. You worked out the kinks and then some."

I've got a laundry list of kinks I'd love to explore with you. Twice.

Stirling looked at him oddly.

Christ, he hadn't said that out loud too, had he?

"It strains my neck to look up at you." She patted the floor beside her. "Come here. Take a load off."

Did everything she say have sexual undertones? Or was he just that fucking perverted?

A voice in the far back of his head warned him this was a bad idea, but the next thing he knew, he was stretched out beside her, staring at the ceiling.

After several long moments, Liam said, "This is weird."

"No it's not. Everything seems weird when you're high."

"Then you're smoking the wrong shit."

"Then so are you because it's *your* shit."

"My shit is premium shit. You said so." He was elated she'd loved the strain he'd entered in the 420 Cup—not that he could tell her that.

"How often do you smoke?" she asked.

"A couple times a week. Mostly at night, to shut off my brain so I can sleep." He wondered if drinkers carried on conversations about their level of booze consumption. "What about you?"

"The same. Unless Jumanji, our excellent budtender, has something new for me to try."

"I still think Jumanji is the worst name to saddle a kid with."

She laughed. "Dude. That is not his real name. Jumanji is his nickname. Anyway, when Jumanji gets excited about a product, then I drop whatever I'm doing and sample the merchandise. It pays to be the boss."

"It pays to have friends in high places."

Stirling groaned. "Bad pun."

"Is there such a thing as a good pun?"

"Of course. But don't ask me for specific examples because I'm pretty baked right now."

He chuckled. "But you're feeling good?"

"Feeling super great. Hungry. I mean, my brain is telling me to eat, not my stomach." She sighed. "You know what I could totally go for right now?"

A huge helping of doc cock?

She said, "A Pop-Tart." A pause. "Do you have any?"

"No. Fresh out. Sorry."

"But you *do* eat them, right?"

"When I was a kid we couldn't afford them. But now I buy them." Not that he could recall the last time he'd done that.

"Good. Because I don't trust anyone who claims they don't like them."

"And the reason behind using Pop-Tarts as a barometer of trustworthiness?"

Stirling snickered. "You want my *Pop*-psychology?"

"That was an excellent pun, you *tarty* little thing."

She started giggling, which cracked him up, and they laughed until they couldn't catch their breath.

"Enough *high*-jinks," he said. She pinched him. "Ow. Finish your explanation about Pop-Tarts used as the gauge to measure sincerity."

"Because there's a flavor to suit everyone's taste buds. Don't like fruity ones? *Bam!* Buy the ones with chocolate. Don't like the chocolate ones? *Bam!* Buy the brown sugar ones. Don't like the frosting? *Bam!* Buy the unfrosted ones. Don't like the sweet ones? *Bam!* Buy the sour fruit ones. There's no excuse, well, beyond having diabetes, for not trying them to find the kind you like best."

Another bizarre stoner conversation that somehow made perfect sense.

Liam felt her looking at him.

"What's your favorite kind of Pop-Tart?"

He kept his gaze trained on the ceiling, racking his brain to find a suitable answer.

"Don't be afraid to tell the truth. No judgment."

"Very favorite? Blue raspberry. Second favorite…frosted cinnamon. Third favorite…the orange creamsicle that was a limited edition one summer."

"Toasted or untoasted?"

"Toasted, of course."

"I think I might love you."

He snorted.

"Guess my favorite kind."

Fuck. He sucked at guessing games; give him facts.

Why are you freaked out? It's a fucking breakfast food *question.*

But even in his hazy state, he understood this meant something important to her. The grocery store shelves appeared in his mind's eye. "I'd guess the corporate woman side of you preferred the brown sugar kind because it seems less juvenile. The dreadlocked woman goes for the s'mores variety first. If the store is out of that, you go with wildberry." He met her eyes. "How did I do?"

"Did you cut the ganja with LSD? Because, dude, it's like you read my mind." Stirling closed her eyes. "What am I thinking about now?"

"That we need to discuss the Macon situation since we're obviously on the same wavelength."

"Nope. I'm thinking your last girlfriend probably didn't eat Pop-Tarts."

"You are correct. No sugar, no gluten, no dairy—"

"No fun," Stirling inserted with a snicker.

"You don't know the half of it."

"So tell me."

Liam faced the ceiling again.

"Come on, I told you about Nick the Prick." When he didn't immediately pour his heart out, Stirling said, "Please? Please, please, please, please, please? With a frosted cherry Pop-Tart on top?"

Jesus. He laughed. "Okay, bulldog. What would you like to know about duck lips?"

"Did she have big tits?"

And...why wasn't he surprised she asked that first? "Yes. Big fake tits. I believe that's a requirement for women in California."

"Was she smart?"

Not as smart as me would come off cocky. Instead, he said, "She wasn't as smart as you."

Silence.

Liam glanced over at her. "What?"

"That was very smooth."

"I have moves, Miss Gradsky, that might even impress you."

"I don't doubt that. So how did you meet Ms. Duck Lips-Fake Tits?"

"Her name is Sera. We worked together." He turned toward Stirling to gauge her reaction.

"Those coworker relationships are a bad idea," she said softly.

"The worst," he agreed. Their faces were so close he could see the indigo-colored ring around her irises.

"They never, ever work out."

"Never." When her focus fell to his lips, for a split second he almost closed the distance between them and kissed her.

Are you even listening to this conversation?

"After the Nick fiasco," she continued, oblivious to his turmoil, "I swore I'd never get intimately involved with a coworker ever again."

"I made the same promise after..." Liam was having a hard time concentrating as he stared into her eyes. God. Could they be any purer blue?

"After...*que Sera, Sera?*"

That broke the spell. He rolled to his back and laughed until he was nearly in tears. He sat up and wiped his glasses.

"Who would've guessed we have the same sense of humor?"

"No one we work with." He shoved his glasses back on. "Speaking of work..."

Stirling groaned. "Five more minutes of no work talk, Mom. Tell me something juicy about your life." Then she rolled to her side, facing away from him.

Instead of becoming annoyed by her avoidance, he launched into the plan of attack he believed to be the most effective in steering Macon into their way of thinking.

Stirling mumbled something, but rather than asking her for clarification, Liam kept going.

Once he drifted into lecture mode, he lost track of time.

A noise permeated his consciousness. He blinked and looked around. Then he checked his watch.

Had he really been lecturing Stirling the past half an hour and she hadn't interrupted him even once? Not even to tell him to can his stuffy professor imitation because she was bored? That wasn't like her at all.

Or maybe you've been staring off into space for thirty minutes and the one-sided conversation only took place in your head.

He heard a noise that sounded like a throaty snort followed by a wheezing whistle. He remained quiet, not entirely sure it wasn't an auditory hallucination.

There it was again. And it was coming from Stirling.

He leaned over her and saw she'd fallen asleep. A post-smoking type of sound sleep. If he tried to rouse her, she'd just be foggy-headed and pissed off that he'd woken her up.

Well, he *had* told her she could crash on his couch. He eyed the distance between the couch and where she looked...pretty damn comfortable on the floor.

Should he sleep on the couch in case she needed something?

Like that huge helping of doc cock?

Yeah, no way could he sleep down here.

Yawning, he pulled his gramma's afghan off the chair and covered her. Then he snagged a small pillow and nestled it next to her head. A couple of her dreadlocks had fallen across her face and he pushed them over her shoulder. He studied her for a moment. The woman was strikingly beautiful. And even after her sweaty workout she had the most intoxicating scent.

Then she snorted like a warthog.

Liam sighed. "If you wake up first, I'm expecting you to make coffee."

He shut off the lights and went upstairs to bed.

Chapter Five

Stirling was late to work.

She was never late.

She hated being late, even when technically she was the boss.

So to combat the guilt for causing her assistant to readjust her schedule, Stirling placed the blame for her tardiness on the broad shoulders of one Dr. Liam Argent.

The last thing she remembered from last night was lying on the floor at Liam's apartment, staring at the patterns in the tin ceiling as she listened to him speak in that deep, sexy voice. A tone so soothing that evidently it had put her right the fuck to sleep. She'd awoken this morning, still on the floor, covered with a crocheted afghan, and a small pillow tucked beneath her head.

No sign of Liam.

Then she heard the pipes rattle above her head. If he'd stepped into the shower, it was time for her to step out. Awkward morning-after chitchat... If she had a chance to avoid it, she would.

She escaped conversation with him, but she didn't escape a parking ticket, nor the morning traffic both going to her place and then to her office.

Stirling kept her sunglasses on as she passed by Shanna's desk, muttering, "Sorry, give me a few minutes."

"Rough night, boss?"

"Weird night," she responded and ducked into her office. She tossed her sunglasses on the desk and her heavy satchel on the visitor's chair.

After draining her coffee, she felt prepared to face the day and summoned Shanna.

Her assistant broke the information into bite-sized pieces so the list wouldn't overwhelm. Stirling jotted notes, asked questions, and thanked the stars she wasn't suffering from a massive hangover because today would be busy.

Shanna paused by the door. "Oh, Dr. Argent stopped by. He said to tell you to come to his lab as soon as you got here."

"When was that?"

"An hour and a half ago."

Hadn't taken him long to get ready this morning. "I'll see him if I have time." If not... Well, she'd never jumped when he summoned her before and she wasn't about to start now.

Around three o'clock, Stirling couldn't ignore her gnawing hunger any longer and headed to the break room. The vending machines were well stocked with a mix of healthy snacks and junk food. She poked the button for baked Cheetos. As soon as she'd retrieved the bag and popped it open, she heard, "The crunchy Cheetos are better."

She jumped, nearly dropping the bag before she whirled around.

Dr. Argent leaned against the wall behind her in the small alcove.

"I see you still prefer to sneak up and scare the crap out of me."

"I see that you still prefer to ignore my meeting requests."

Stirling pointed at him with a Cheeto. "Requests I'll consider. Demands...not so much."

"Regardless. We need to talk before our meeting with Macon."

"What meeting?" She shoved a couple of Cheetos in her mouth and crunched. God. She could eat like four bags of these.

His eyes narrowed. "Do you remember *anything* we talked about last night?"

"Yes. I remember everything until I fell asleep."

"That's funny, because we discussed a specific strategy for the meeting today. And you clearly weren't asleep because you hadn't started snoring yet."

"Hah!" She pointed another Cheeto at him. "Now I know you're lying because I don't snore."

Half a heartbeat later, Dr. Speedy was in her face. "You snore like a freakin' asthmatic bulldog. I'd intended to crash on the couch in case you woke up disoriented, but the cacophony kept me awake."

"So you retired to your nice, comfy bed and left me to sleep on the hard wood floor?" she retorted.

Guilt momentarily flashed in his eyes, then he banked it. "Didn't seem to affect you because you slept like—"

"Someone had given me a hit of super-indica sleep aid?" she shot back.

"You could've said no to that last hit. As a matter of fact, maybe you should have."

The challenge she read in his eyes? She was a weed lightweight. As. If. "And miss the chance to burn through your private stash of premium ganja? That is the height of rudeness in the smoking culture."

"Yes, it is." Liam leaned forward and bit the tip of the Cheeto she'd been brandishing at him.

"Hey!" He'd moved in close enough she could distinguish each one of his long, dark eyelashes. He was a remarkable looking man. With killer lips.

"But the very pinnacle of rudeness is when you're spilling your life story to the pain-in-the-ass coworker who demanded the 'juicy' details and then she falls into a drooling, snoring coma."

Stirling's gaze zoomed back to his. "I really did that?"

"Within the first five minutes."

"Dammit, Liam, I am so sorry."

"Was I boring you?"

"I don't think so. But I honestly don't remember when I dozed off. I just remember being in that floaty place with the perfect cadence of your voice pulling me under."

He blinked at her. "You like the sound of my voice?"

"When you don't sound like a douchebag know-it-all."

"I suppose I could say the same to you."

"You did last night, remember?"

Liam frowned. "I did?"

"Yes. You said my husky voice sounded like raw sex."

"*I* said that to you?"

I think so. She nodded.

They stared at each other. But it was a more curious stare-down than aggressive.

Stirling glanced away first. "I *am* sorry. Do I get another chance to hear all about Dr. Liam's Livin' Large life?"

"Nope." He sucked the last half of the Cheeto—and her fingers—into his mouth.

It shouldn't have been sexy, but goddamn it was. Her fingers, her hand—her whole damn arm tingled.

"Finish your snack, Miss Gradsky, and be in my office in fifteen minutes."

She smiled up at him. In an inspired moment of contrariness, she wiped her cheese-coated lips right below his name embroidered on the front of his pristine white lab coat.

His look of shock?

Priceless.

She ducked under his arm, tossing off a breezy "I'll consider it," and sailed out of the break room.

* * * *

In hindsight, maybe she shouldn't have taunted him.

Ten minutes after she returned to her office, he called Shanna to remind her that Miss Gradsky had an immediate meeting with Dr. Argent.

A call Shanna didn't bother to put through...the first five times.

When all four office lines were ringing at once, as well as Stirling's cell phone exploding with text messages every ten seconds from Dr. Determined, she gave in.

Maybe she stomped her cowgirl boots down every tile hallway so he could hear her coming.

She didn't bother using her keycard to gain access to his lab; she just pressed on the call button. As she sang the tune of *Mary Had a Little Lamb* in her head, her finger kept time poking the buzzer.

Dr. Annoying came personally to let her in. "Ah, Miss Gradsky. How fortuitous that you're attending this meeting."

"Yes, it's gonna be super-fun. Thanks for having me."

He directed her into his private office, a space she hadn't been allowed in before.

Weird. He didn't have a normal desk; the man had a treadmill desk. Of course Dr. Efficient wouldn't want to waste precious time by actually, oh...sitting down like a normal human.

Behind the work-exercise torture device was an oversized loveseat in bland brown. A compact conference table, littered with papers, catalogues, and Post-it notes had been moved in front of it.

He gestured to the couch. "Have a seat."

"I'm thinking I'd rather run on the treadmill. That way I'll be sure to get my cardio in today."

His laughter rang out and Stirling found herself grinning.

When he said, "Stirling, can you please not fight me on every goddamned thing?" she wasn't even provoked by it.

"Fine. But you better have laid in a supply of refreshments for this convergence."

"I have Diet Mountain Dew or Red Bull." He adjusted his glasses. "I didn't have time to create an appetizer plate of edibles, but your recent bag of Cheetos should hold you over."

She squinted at his lab coat. No orange smear. "Seriously? You had to change lab coats this late in the day because of a small stain? Dr. OCD much?"

"It's the same lab coat. The stain is gone because I used a Tide bleach pen on it." His gaze lingered on the orange spot above her left breast. "You should try one sometime."

"Pass. I ditched my laundry pens the same time I ditched the business suits. I'll have a Diet Dew."

He tossed her a can, grabbed a Red Bull for himself, and sat next to her. "Before we get into the upcoming meeting with Macon, I need to know why you stormed out yesterday. It seemed an over-the-top reaction considering what we were discussing."

Stirling leaned back into the cushion. "I told you part of it last night. Macon sued GenAgra and got me a high seven-figure settlement."

Liam's eyebrow rose. "That's...unusual, isn't it?"

"Very. Macon uncovered a couple of other situations with GenAgra where female executives were 'unjustly released' and their severance packages didn't reflect that they were basically blackballed in the industry. Macon couldn't prevent me from being blackballed, so he forced their hand for maximum payout. GenAgra didn't want to be crucified in the court of public opinion."

"So they settled with you rather than taking their chances in court with Macon."

"Yes. Taxes ate up a good chunk of the settlement. Most lawyers would've taken forty percent off the top. But I pitched Macon the idea of investing the fees I owed him in an organic farm." She popped the top on her can. "He countered my idea with his; invest my settlement money into the cannabis business. Since Macon owned a medical dispensary—through default after one of his clients went bankrupt—

he'd had a foot in the cannabis industry and a guaranteed slot for recreational sales. During the two years that the legalities of recreational cannabis sales were worked out, we bought a building complex. Macon handled the contractors that retrofitted the back building into a grow house with state-of-the-art watering and fertilization equipment as well as ventilation and various lighting systems."

"What were you doing during that time?" he said tightly.

Stirling met his angry gaze head-on. "What is your problem?"

"Did your brother railroad you into going into this business by holding the capital you'd been awarded hostage?"

"No. As happy as I was to end my association with GenAgra, I didn't know what to do with myself or the money. For my entire adult life I'd either been studying or working. And we had time until we could get the recreational business rolling—intentional pun—so we could do it right from the start." She grinned when he laughed. "Careful, I might believe you secretly like my sense of humor."

"It's refreshing that you have one. Go on."

Refreshing? What an odd word choice. "So for one thing, he sent me to Cannabis U in Amsterdam." She gave him a curious look. "Have you ever been?"

"I've taught a few seminars there."

She bumped her shoulder into his. "Of course the god of ganja, the cannabis creator of 'Livin' Large' probably has a dedicated suite and golden pot leaf on the Weed Wall of Fame."

Liam blinked those gorgeous silvery eyes at her.

"What?"

"So you're this chatty and cute when you're not high?"

What the fuck?

He said I was cute?

"Which, I might add, is far better than you being your usual belligerent and bratty self."

Belligerent and bratty? That seemed less offensive than cute.

"But you only seem to be belligerent and bratty around me. Why is that?"

A pause stretched.

"Stirling?" he prompted.

"Oh, you're allowing *cute* little ol' me to speak now? Excuse me while I skip to my magical closet and don my fluffy pink tutu and sparkly unicorn crown before I give you my cutesy answer."

He pointed at her with his Red Bull can. "And there's Stirling number three, sarcastic and defensive."

"The not-quite-insults are...insulting. You can do better."

"Stop skirting the real question." Liam leaned closer. "The truth. No bullshit."

"What exactly do you want to know?"

"During your tirade yesterday with your brother, you said this wasn't what you signed on for. Sounded to me like Macon used coercion to get you to invest. And I am not okay with that, Stirling. Not at all."

"Let's back up. What bait did my brother use to lure *you* here?"

"Just that I'd be working in Colorado in the legalized cannabis business."

Something about that answer didn't ring true. "And you just signed on?"

"I needed the change. You never finished telling me if you just gave up your intention to start an organic farm after Macon offered you a different option."

"No, that's still on the horizon. Part of the deal with Macon was I'd stay in business with him long enough to earn back my investment. He'd made it sound like this cannabis business would be in the black and turning a profit within two years. Yesterday was the first time he's admitted he knew it'd be a longer time frame. So I wonder if it's smart to leave the land fallow for four years."

"Wait. You already own the land?"

"Yes. My parents cut me a deal on two hundred acres bordering their ranch. I bought it before we incorporated High Society, due to the federal restrictions on investing 'illegally obtained capital' and the land would be subject to seizure. A year ago I was about to start the process of getting the official organic certification and I hit a major snag."

"What kind of snag?"

"Macon brought in some expert in biodiversity and he claimed that to bring the soil up to standards we'd need a three-part process. The first was to do nothing for a year. I'll admit, I was so disappointed in that verdict that I tuned out the other two recommendations and focused on High Society."

"Why was *Macon* involved in fielding experts for *your* future organic farm?"

Stirling looked at him strangely. Where had this sudden terseness come from?

Oh right. Hello, Dr. Jekyll.

"Why? Because he's my brother and my business partner. He offered to help me since he was in the Denver area. I wasn't. I'd been staying at home—our family homestead in southeastern Colorado—to deal with ranch matters while my parents were relocating and building the rodeo school." She studied the hard set to his jaw. "Why are you so pissy about this? It doesn't concern you."

"Yes, it does." He shot to his feet and began to pace, muttering to himself.

"Liam. What is going on?"

"*I'm* the biodiversity expert that Macon hired."

"What?"

"Macon brought me up here a year ago to assess two hundred acres where he planned to grow organic cannabis."

"Is this another one of your pranks?" she demanded.

"No." Liam flopped back on the couch with a heavy sigh. "I wouldn't joke about that. And I sure as hell don't want you to hate me more than you already do."

"Tough shit. Start talking."

By the time Liam finished his side of the story, Stirling's head throbbed.

Liam let her organize her thoughts. "Why would your brother mislead me into believing he owned the land I inspected?"

"Because he could."

"That's not an answer."

"But a couple of strange things happened around that time now make sense." She turned sideways on the couch to face him. "Do you remember about a month after we first started working together we attended the open house for my parents' rodeo school?"

"Ah, the night from hell. Macon informed me of my required attendance at the event, then he pawned me off on you. You drove as if you were auditioning for *The Fast and the Furious* through Denver traffic, intentionally ditching me."

"Hey, it's not my fault that your fuel efficient car can't keep up with a V-10. Anyway, remember Cres Grant? The hot cowboy I asked to hit on you to check my gaydar?"

"Like I could forget that." He cocked his head. "This story does have a point?"

"Yes. I'm putting the pieces together as I go. So, a couple of months later, Cres's boyfriend Breck approached me at another one of my parents' parties and remarked it was unfortunate the Ag land wasn't ready for development."

"Leading you to believe that Macon had hired *Breck* as the biodiversity expert," Liam finished.

Stirling touched her nose. "Then Breck apologized for passing on the job offer from Macon, but he couldn't wait for us to get the organic farm on track. Instead, he'd taken a job with the state inspecting livestock. That never clicked until now."

Liam scowled. "I believed Macon was different, but he's just another slimy lawyer, who apparently would even fuck over his own sister."

"Not true. Macon would never do that."

"How can you defend him?" he demanded.

She counted to ten before she answered. "Look. I'm not defending him, just... Let me explain him. Macon has always looked out for himself first. He invested twice as much capital in High Society as I did. He needed me focused on *this* venture, not one a few years down the road that might not be a viable business anyway. So I understand his reason for doing it."

"With this Breck guy? Or with me?"

"Both. At that time, Breck was considering leaving to find permanent employment. Macon probably made up the promise of a job to keep Breck around so he wouldn't run away from his feelings for Cres. They're happy and together, so Macon's heart was in the right place."

"And what about me?"

"Macon brought you to Denver and gave you a sneak peek at my land, so you'd believe he'd eventually have a large-scale cannabis business. He must've had doubts that you'd sign on with such a small company if there wasn't room for expansion." She scrutinized the rigidness of his body as he continued to pace. "How long did it take you to officially sign on after Macon promised he'd custom design a lab for you?"

"One hour," he said without hesitation. "And it pains me to admit that, even as I applaud your brother for playing me so expertly." He ran a hand through his hair. "I wanted out of my contract. I needed an attorney with a successful track record in breaking complex employment contracts and a mutual friend recommended him. We had several phone conversations before I agreed to come to Denver. That's when he pulled that… Hey, while you're here—and before I share the good news about your contract—could you check out this land for me and give me your professional opinion?" He laughed harshly. "So I did. Not knowing it wasn't his land. But at least he told you the truth about my recommendation to leave the land fallow for at least a year. Anyway, he assured me he'd found a loophole that would end my employment with GreenTech and allow me to go to work for him at High Society without restrictions."

"And to sweeten the pot—ha-ha pardon the pun—he offered you full autonomy?"

His gaze sharpened. "How did—"

"It's how Macon operates." She heaved a heavy sigh. "He's not malicious, but he is the king of manipulation. I'd unleash my fury on him if I thought he'd acted out of spite. But he did what he had to do to make all of the pieces fit where he wanted them to. I hate to admit it, but he's been successful in every endeavor *because* he finds a way to make things work for him."

They both chewed that over.

Stirling sighed again. "But knowing all of this doesn't change anything."

"That's where you're wrong." He downed his Red Bull. "Ironically enough, that's also where you checked out of our conversation last night."

"Let's pretend for a moment that I don't have the faintest clue as to what you're talking about. Oh right, I *don't* have to pretend."

Liam reached into his mini fridge and pulled out two cans of…

"Cannabis cola?" she read out loud. "Seriously?"

"Yes. We need clear and calm heads. This will do it. While we're both sipping sativa syrup, you'll listen to the strategy I've laid out for Macon."

"Fine, Dr. Devious, you have my attention."

"We convince him to buy the biggest industrial CO2 extraction equipment on the market."

"Go big or go home, right?"

"Exactly. I already know how to operate the machinery. The key is to emphasize almost immediate cash flow—assuming the permits are issued in a timely fashion, the installation is quick, the company techs arrive on site and refresh my memory on specific instrumentation, and there isn't a backlog on the various inspections we'll need. Everything you said in the meeting yesterday is inarguable."

She didn't mask her look of shock. "We're in agreement on something important for once?"

"It appears that way. But the trick is keeping the combative status quo between us. Because if Macon suspects we're on the same side *against* him—"

"He'll never agree to give us the green light."

"Precisely."

"Or option B…I could just write a company check and we can play the 'Oops, I thought I told you about that major equipment purchase' card."

"I considered that angle. But subterfuge is his preferred methodology with us; we'll see how well it works on him."

Liam insisted they do a practice run involving all three scenarios he'd planned for.

Twenty minutes later, they were as ready as they'd ever be. Silence stretched between them as they drank their sodas and let the plan sink in.

"Any questions?"

She shook her head.

"You seem nervous."

"I am. I don't normally use trickery to get what I want and it feels wrong."

"You use trickery all the time." He drained his soda and crushed the can. "Remember all those pranks you played on me? Keep them in mind when we're with Macon. It'll make you feel superior. And if that doesn't work? Think about how much you hate me."

Here was a make or break moment. "Liam, I don't hate you."

His eyebrow winged up in a silent, mocking "Oh really?"

"In fact, I told you last night I loved you." She nudged his leg with hers. "Remember that?"

"It's a bit hazy. Was that during our scintillating conversation about Pop-Tarts? Or right before you went comatose during my soliloquy?"

Cocky asshat. "Both." She smiled. "From the moment you strolled in here, you've acted uptight and holier-than-thou. It reminded me of *me* a few years ago and I hated the reminder. Then you were stubborn about cooperating with me—"

"Or you refused to do things my way, as I saw it," he interjected, "but go on."

"And I started pranking you, expecting you'd ignore it. But you embraced it. You even surpassed me on a few occasions. So..." *Shut up, Stirling. You've already said too much.*

"So...?" he prompted.

"I was surprised you gave as good as you got."

His gaze encompassed her face before he trained his focus entirely on her lips.

"What?"

"You have no idea how much I want to prove how good I can give it to you."

Boom. It was as if a thunderclap cleared the air between them, leaving energy crackling in the space, buzzing and ready for lightning to strike at any moment.

"Stirling."

That voice. Pure sex. Her mind screamed at her to retreat, but her body, lulled by the warmth of his muscular leg pressing into hers, refused to budge. "But...you've always acted like I'm beneath you."

"I've always wanted you beneath me." He angled his head until his mouth touched the spot below her ear.

She didn't want to break the spell, but she trembled when his lips journeyed down the side of her neck. "I didn't think you were attracted to me," she said on a near whisper.

"And I didn't think you were an idiot, Miss Gradsky."

Stirling froze.

Then Liam was nose to nose with her, his eyes fierce behind his glasses. "You are a beautiful woman. Stunningly beautiful when you smile, cunningly beautiful when you've got that devious look in your eyes. You're intelligent and clever, and I'd be a fool not to be attracted to you."

"And you, Dr. Liam Argent, are no fool," she whispered.

"Exactly." He smiled. "So the question is... What do we do about it?"

Take a step back?

Or take a leap of faith?

Stirling didn't hesitate as she felt the rush of solid ground disappearing beneath her. "We do this," she murmured as she brushed her lips across his. Then she curled her hand around the back of his neck and brought him even closer. "And a whole lot of this."

Their mouths collided. The soft exploration of lips gave way to a teasing of tongues. Then hunger—sweet, hot, desperate hunger overtook them both. Mouth on mouth, their heads changing angles in perfect synchronicity to taste deeper, to better sate this need. The exchange of breath and the wet glide of lips... This wasn't a mere kiss. This was a promise of intimacy on a whole different level.

As one they broke the kiss, but their lips weren't more than a millimeter apart.

They had about ten seconds of staring into each other's eyes with identical *holy shit* expressions, when a buzzing started beneath her right breast.

Wait. When had she climbed onto Liam's lap?

"That's my phone."

She leaned back and watched as he fished his cell out of the front pocket of his lab coat.

"It's Macon." He answered "Hey" without looking away from Stirling. A few moments later he said, "Uh-huh." Pause. "Uh-huh." Longer pause. "Uh-huh."

She smirked. She'd never heard Dr. Vocabulary utter *uh-huh* even once the past ten months, to say nothing of it being his only verbal response. Good to know that kiss flustered him as much as it had her.

He hung up and continued to stare at her through his fogged-up lenses.

"Liam?"

"Uh-huh."

Snort. "What did Macon want?"

He blinked rapidly a couple of times. "He's here, ready to meet with us."

"Okay. I'll just—"

"Wait." Liam pressed his lips to hers. Once. Twice. Then he said softly, "Don't dismiss this. Please."

The tenderness in his words and his kiss made her ache. "I won't." She stood and straightened her blouse. "I need to stop at my office first. So I'll, ah...see you there."

"Remember how we're going to play this."

Right. I'm having a hard time remembering my own damn name because I want to play with you.

She grabbed her soda can and hightailed it out of there.

With that mind-blowing kiss stuck on replay in her head, she was caught completely off guard when she heard, "Where have you been?"

A gasp escaped when she spun around and saw Macon lounging against the wall across from her office. "Oh. Hey." *Nothing to see here, bro. I wasn't just sucking face with my supposed nemesis.*

His gaze sharpened. "Why the guilty look, sis?"

Shit.

"Whatcha hiding in your hand?"

She held up the can of cannabis cola and grinned sheepishly. "I'm afraid I needed liquid courage before this meeting."

"I'm not going to reprimand you. In fact, where did you get that? I could use one."

"Ah... Sorry. It was the last one in my fridge but the retail store sells them."

"All right. I'll grab one and see you in the conference room."

Chapter Six

Liam didn't move as he watched the door to his office close behind Stirling.

No, he wasn't rattled at all.

He remained Dr. Calm, Cool, and Collected, same as always.

Is that right? So why is your body shaking? Why is your heart thundering. Why is your face burning? Why is your cock as hard as a test tube?

Fuck. He was a mess after kissing Stirling. A hormonal wreck—he'd almost said "screw it" to the meeting in favor of screwing her. He imagined pushing her skirt up, holding her ass in his hands, feeling her cowgirl boots digging into the backs of his thighs as his cock pounded into her.

He ditched his glasses and scrubbed his hands over his face.

Okay, man, focus on something besides how her hunger matches yours. Or how soft her lips remained as you kissed the shit out of each other. Or how she plastered her chest against yours. Or how there wasn't an iota of regret in those lust-filled eyes when the kiss ended.

He'd be rubbing one out to the memory of that kiss for weeks to come.

Liam stood on wobbly legs and threw out a hand to the countertop beside him. The potency of Stirling's kisses on top of the cannabis cola… No wonder he wasn't stable. His world had been flipped upside down.

He didn't bother checking his appearance in the mirror as he jammed his hands through his hair. He cleaned his glasses and collected the paperwork he'd need. After one last look around his office, he left.

Artie caught him halfway down the hall. "Hey, Doc. You got time to look at weird spots I found on two of the plants in the stage-one grow?"

Liam stopped. "You isolated the plants in question?"

"Course I did. Then I went back through and checked all the other plants but I didn't see any others had been infected—if that's what this is."

"Any ideas what it might be, Artie?"

He scratched his beard. "Nope."

"I'm late to a meeting with the Gradskys. I don't know how long it'll last. Will you be around for a while?"

Artie shook his head. "It's my granddaughter's birthday party tonight."

"Who is on second shift?"

"George. But I'll be back tomorrow at noon."

"I'll check them before I go home. Tell curious George not to mess with those plants." George, the young, overly enthusiastic assistant grower, tended to act first, ask questions later.

"Already warned him, Doc." Artie grinned. "Don't see you carrying a bat to your meeting. Have you and Stirling settled your differences?"

Liam flashed back to Stirling's nails digging into the back of his neck as she kissed him. "We're trying new ways to communicate."

"Well, good luck to ya. That wildcat needs a firm hand to tame her."

I don't want to tame her. I like the way she hisses and claws, and how much sweeter will it be if I get that wildcat to purr from my touch?

"Doc?"

He blinked. Christ, he had it bad if he couldn't even hold a five-minute conversation without thinking about her. "Have a good night, Artie."

The door to the conference room was open. Stirling was alone, sitting at the head of the table.

Déjà vu hit him…they'd been in this same scenario yesterday.

She glanced up as he walked in.

Macon bumped into him from behind. "What's the holdup, Argent? Move it."

"Impatient much?"

Stirling hadn't looked away from Liam—granted, that meant he hadn't looked away from her either.

Don't blush, don't smile at me, and don't give us away.

Her gaze flicked to her brother. "Hooray. Another meeting with Dweedle Dee and Dweedle Dum."

Relief allowed him to breathe again. He took the same seat beside her as yesterday. "That's not a very flattering way to refer to yourself, Miss Gradsky."

"Hilarious, Dr. Deadpan."

Macon sighed. "Knock it off. I'm not in the mood for the bicker twins today."

"You're the one who called the meeting," Liam pointed out.

"I did. And first off, I need to apologize, Stirling. I was an ass to you and I became a defensive jackass when you asked questions about things that you, as my partner, should already have the answers to."

"Apology accepted."

That happened much quicker than Liam had anticipated. He almost wished she would've made Macon sweat it out.

"I don't blame the drop in profits on you. I looked at the number of employee hours in the retail store, which is higher than I'd like."

Stirling started to argue.

Macon held up his hand. "So I agree that we need to hire a manager. His or her salary wouldn't increase the overall amount of wage payout if we cull other employee hours."

Stirling jumped up, went to the window, and pulled the curtain back.

"What in the hell are you doing?" Macon asked.

"Seeing if there's a full moon or a comet or a falling star because you actually listened to me and agreed with me. It's a rare occurrence."

Macon rolled his eyes. "I'm not the bad guy, just the bottom-line guy."

"I'll set up interviews for managers. But if I don't feel any of the applicants are a good fit, I'd like to hire from within."

"Who?"

"Cheney."

Liam frowned. "The girl with gigantic gauges who always wears that 'Fuck the patriarchy' T-shirt to meetings?"

"I'd wear the T-shirt, too, if my parents named me after that vice president," Stirling said.

"Instead, your parents named you after silverware. And they misspelled it," Liam said drolly.

"For your information, Dr. Geography *Fail*, I'm named after a city in Ireland," she retorted.

"Enough. Jesus," Macon complained. "Back to the issue. I trust your judgment, Stirling. Hire whomever you like. I'm glad I won't be around to listen to you two. I will, however, warn the other employees to wear earplugs when you start working together."

"Excuse me? Us"—Liam gestured to Stirling, then himself— "working together?"

"Yes. You're not the only whiz at research, Argent. Last night I studied the projected output on the supercritical CO_2 extraction machine you're both so gung-ho about and I agree, it's an excellent sideways step to increase profit. I contacted a dealer this morning. They have a used machine for sale for half the retail price, so I agreed to buy it and the vacuum ovens from him. It'll all be here Monday. I called in a couple of favors regarding the MIPS—Marijuana Infused Permits—and supposedly we're on the fast track for city services inspection. But that means construction to bring the room to code will begin Tuesday. After all that is done, the technicians from the company will be onsite to set the calibrations and troubleshoot any issues. So starting next week, you two will be working very closely together."

Stirling blurted out, "Absolutely not. No way."

Jesus, Stirling, don't oversell it. This is what we want.

While Macon said, "Hang on," and checked his cell phone, Liam willed Stirling to look at him.

When she did, he gave an imperceptible shake of his head.

Then Macon jumped back into the conversation. "I have to go. I got a client who landed in jail." He stood. "Any questions?"

"Why did you change your mind?" Liam asked.

"Because you both indicated it was a necessary purchase. I figured if the bickering twins, who never agreed on a damn thing the past ten months, were in agreement about this, then it likely had merit. Keep me informed. After I prevent numbnuts from spending the weekend in the drunk tank, I'm off to a ten-day international law seminar in Geneva."

"You're going to Switzerland?" Stirling aped. "Just like that?"

"I doubt he was referring to Geneva, Alabama, Miss Geography Fail," Liam responded.

Stirling's hard look warned him not to oversell it either.

Macon picked up his briefcase. "Last thing. Next Saturday night there's this thing for London. I agreed to do my DJ spin, but that ain't happening since I'll be out of the country. So you have to take over,

Stirl."

"What? No! I suck at that 'be witty on the fly' stuff, Macon." She glared at Liam. "Not one word of agreement."

Why didn't this woman think she was funny? She always had a quick comeback and she cracked him up. Liam held his hands in the air in silent surrender.

"I'll have my secretary email you the playlist. It's easy. You'll do great." Macon came around and kissed her cheek. "Behave, little sis, and maybe I'll bring you back a Swiss watch." Macon tipped his chin at Liam and hustled out.

"I'm expecting a Patek Philippe!" Stirling yelled as the door slammed behind him.

"I don't think he heard you."

Neither of them moved nor spoke, even though they sat right next to each other.

Finally Liam got up and grabbed a bottled water. "Want one?"

"Yes. Please."

He said, "Are you okay?"

"That was one scenario that we hadn't expected," Stirling said. "Or maybe Macon has your office bugged and the sneaky bastard knew what we had planned?"

Liam shook his head. "I regularly sweep the lab for bugs."

"Paranoid much?"

"I'm very distrustful, courtesy of what I dealt with at my previous job."

"Will you tell me about it? Maybe...over dinner?"

He leaned closer. "Are you propositioning me, Miss Gradsky?"

"Yes. Pajamas and a toothbrush are optional."

Seeing that sexy curve to her lower lip and the heat in her eyes, Liam understood he hadn't stood a chance against her. She had IT. That elusive appeal he couldn't verbally define but physically affected him like a shot of adrenaline. "Can I just say something first?"

"If you must."

"You are so fucking hot."

She released a husky laugh. "Not what I expected, but I'll take it."

"My inner seventeen-year-old boy is in awe that you're even talking to geeky us."

"What is the hot, sexy man I'm staring at right now thinking?"

Liam twined a dreadlock around his finger. "That I can't wait to wrap this hair around my hand as I'm fucking you from behind."

Stirling's grin widened. "You're not prim and proper when the lab coat comes off, are you?"

"Not. Even. Fucking. Close."

"So this persona you present of polite reserve?"

"Is my professional side." He tugged her closer by that hank of hair and slid his hand up the inside of her thigh. "I save my dirty talk and filthy fantasies for after working hours."

She spread her legs wider and brushed those cherry red lips across his. "Show me."

"Are you sure you can handle it? I've been told my needs are...intense."

"How ironic." Stirling's fingers circled his wrist and she pulled his hand right between her legs. "I've been told I put the 'ho' in boho."

He groaned. "Are you always going to try and top me?"

She smiled against his mouth. "Every single chance I get."

"Let's go."

Liam allowed one hard kiss before retreating. He gathered the paperwork he hadn't needed. "Are you finished for the day?"

"Yes. How about you?"

"I have to check on something Artie asked me about. It shouldn't take long."

"I'll text you my address." As Stirling sauntered by, she palmed his ass. "Fair warning, hot stuff. The only drooling I'll be doing tonight will be on your cock."

He just sort of stood there like a dumbass as she walked out the door.

A dumbass with a hard-on about to get lucky, so move it, Einstein.

Liam locked up the lab and stashed his stuff in his car before he headed for the grow house. He swiped his keycard and punched in his code when the green light flashed.

Heat and the pungent scent of cannabis hit him as soon as he stepped inside.

George was right there, handing Liam a lab apron and gloves. "Hey, Doc. Artie said you'd be by."

He donned the protective gear and said, "I'll let you know if I need anything."

"Cool. I'll just be working."

Liam opened the door to the stage-one grow and squinted. Not only had humidity fogged his glasses, but the lights were blinding—as they needed to be in this eighteen hours of daylight stage. As soon as his eyes and his glasses adjusted, he scanned the room. It wasn't filled with plants, which wasn't right. They'd figured out the amount of useable grow space to the nearest inch. So why wasn't it all being used?

Maybe the better question is why don't you know the answer to that?

He ducked beneath the plastic flap that separated the chemical and tool room. The two plants were in the corner. Even from here they appeared dehydrated.

First he examined them with just his naked eye. Then he used a 30X battery-powered magnifier to scrutinize every leaf joint, leaf, and section of the stem from the dirt up. Besides the spots on the lower leaves, no immediate issue jumped out at him, but he had his suspicions.

Using his phone, he snapped close-ups of the plant and texted them to his friend Dougie. He'd been growing his own for twenty years, in every climate imaginable; he was the real ganja guru.

Less than three minutes later his cell rang. "Hey D, what's up?"

"What am I looking at?" Dougie asked.

Liam explained. Then he asked, "Any ideas?"

"My first thought was powdery mildew."

Mine too. "But?"

"But have you checked any of the other plants in the same grow room?"

"No. Artie said these were the only two."

Dougie laughed. "Never take anyone's word for it. Do a random check and call me back."

Grumbling to himself, Liam returned to the grow room and pulled three plants from different areas. Upon closer examination they didn't look better than the two isolated plants; they looked worse.

All three of them.

In a panic, Liam checked the entire first row of plants. The leaves were droopy; the lower branches had leaves covered in spots and white residue.

How the fuck hadn't Artie—or anyone else—noticed this?

He stepped back. Wait a second. With the way the plants were crowded together, and the super bright lights, the spots and white residue were invisible to the naked eye.

Fuck.

He snapped more pics and sent them off.

This time Dougie called back in under a minute. "Dude. That *is* powdery mildew and that's bad, bad news. Those spots and the white powder only show up *after* the plant has been infected for a couple of weeks."

"Jesus, I know that," Liam snapped.

"They didn't teach you how to diagnose a diseased plant or how to contain a major outbreak when they gave you that fancy degree, *Dr. Argent?*" Dougie asked snidely.

His old-school pothead friend never let him live it down that he'd gone to college to learn to do what Dougie already knew. "I've studied it and isolated it on individual plants, but nothing on this level. So yes, you have expertise that I don't. Has this happened to you?"

Dougie sighed. "About a year after I increased the number of plants I was growing, I noticed the leaves looked droopy. I assumed I needed to up the amount of water and increase the humidity level. By the time I realized that my solution had fed the disease instead of reversed it, it was too damn late. I lost the entire crop."

He slumped against the partition. They were looking at a loss of half a million dollars or more.

Christ. He wanted to throw up.

"Liam? Bud, what can I do to help?"

"Can you come down here? Diagnosis will take half as long with two of us." And frankly at this point, he didn't trust any of the employees to help because how had they missed this?

What's really eating at you…is how did you *miss it? It's your job. You should've caught it.*

"Then what happens? If the entire crop is dusted?" Dougie prompted.

"I need to call in MED to document and witness us destroying the plants."

"Fucking Marijuana Enforcement Division. I'll help you tonight, but I'm jetting when those nosy bastards show up."

"Deal."

Liam hung up, cracked open the door to the next stage grow, and yelled, "George!"

"What's up, Doc?"

Don't snarl at him. "We've got widespread contamination in here. Shut this door, lock it, and implement contamination protocol. You remember what that entails?"

"Uh, yes."

"Do it."

Liam shut and locked the door from his side. Then he dropped the plastic sheeting down around all four walls and changed the security code so the emergency exit could be used without triggering an alarm.

Then he made the phone call he was dreading.

Stirling answered right away. "Hey, are you running late?"

"I feel like running away."

"What's going on?"

Without preamble, he informed her of the situation in the detail he was known for.

It was excruciating to wait for her reaction.

Finally, she said, "What do you need me to do? Help identify the diseased plants?"

"No. At this point I think it's best if Dougie, my…source and I do that part. The less chance for contamination elsewhere, the better."

"But Liam, this process will take you hours and hours."

"Good thing there's a coffeepot in here." He looked at his feet. "Jesus, Stirling. I'm sorry about all of this."

"It's not your fault."

"Isn't it? I'm the cannabis expert. I should've been, oh, keeping a better eye on the cannabis, don't you agree?"

"Beat yourself up later, Dr. Doom. I'll be pacing with my phone for the rest of the night, so don't hesitate to call if you need anything. Okay? Promise me."

"I promise. There are a few things you can do for me."

"Name them."

He closed his eyes and made a mental list. "Do you have a piece of paper handy?"

"I'll grab one."

Liam rattled off everything that might be an issue in the next twenty-four hours. He probably went overboard, but he knew Stirling would want to deal with the minutiae, not just the major problems.

"I'll keep you up to date as much as I can."

"Take care. Be safe. I'm a phone call away."

He hung up and got to work.

Well, he wouldn't have to worry about confessing to Stirling that his contract with High Society was only for a year—because when the lost income numbers rolled in, Macon would fire his ass.

* * * *

Late Sunday afternoon…

Watching half a million dollars burn…the queasiness in his stomach wasn't from the smoke.

Two MED officers stood on either side of the barrel. One took pictures of every part of the plant. The other one documented the destruction, including stripping off the RFID tags.

As co-owner, Stirling had to sign her agreement that nothing fraudulent was taking place. She'd acted as somber as he'd ever seen her.

A private security guard—a burly biker, bald headed, covered in tattoos, and wearing a cut that declared him a member of Grinder Kings motorcycle club—also witnessed the burn.

Liam had a moment of panic when the dude showed up late Saturday night with a sleeping bag and a lawn chair, barking at Liam to get some sleep, under Stirling's orders. Then he told Liam to lock himself in; he and his "brothers" would secure the building until MED arrived in the morning. After being up for almost forty-eight hours, Liam crawled in the sleeping bag and crashed.

They were down to the last couple of plants. He looked around at the eerily empty grow house. It'd remain empty until MED closed the case and gave the green light to replant. The only saving grace in this situation was the destroyed crop was medicinal, not recreational. Since seventy percent of their plants were required to only be for medicinal use, and the latest P&L indicated medicinal sales were down, it could've been much worse.

After the barrels containing the plant matter were loaded, Liam watched the MED van drive off.

The biker spoke to Stirling before he roared away on his Harley, leaving Liam and Stirling alone.

She crossed the gravel parking lot and stood in front of him.

Would she punch him? Yell at him? Fire him?

Those wise blue eyes took his measure for several long moments and then she wrapped her arms around him, pressing her cheek to his chest.

Not what he'd expected but he'd take it.

They stayed locked together until Stirling tipped her head back and said, "Come home with me."

"You're sure?"

"Yes. If you go home alone you'll spend the rest of the day on your laptop, obsessively researching why this happened, and you'll get no rest at all."

"Maybe I *should* stay awake, racked with guilt."

"See?" She jabbed her finger into his chest. "That's what I mean. We'll deal with the timeline of how it happened and create protocol for the future...tomorrow."

Liam rested his forehead to hers. "All right. But I need to stop at my place first and get out of these clothes."

"Then we'll just go there. Besides utter lack of Pop-Tarts, you probably have more food than I do." She smiled slyly. "And I know you've got better weed."

Chapter Seven

Stirling took Liam's suggestion to make herself at home by rummaging through his closet while he showered. So his shocked look when he found her barefoot in his kitchen wearing his shirt made her laugh.

"What? I was cold."

"Aren't you supposed to strut around in my shirt the morning after?"

She shrugged. "I'm not so much with following societal norms anymore."

"And she gets an 'atta girl' for that." His rapt gaze roamed over her as he crowded her against the counter. "Dreadlocks suit you. There's nothing to detract from this beautiful face."

I can't wait to wrap this hair around my hand as I'm fucking you from behind. Remembering the sexy, matter-of-fact way he'd stated that still gave her shivers. Had she truly found the man who accepted—and approved of—all parts of her? Physical and intellectual?

His rough-skinned knuckles followed the curve of her jaw. "I was really looking forward to our Friday night together."

"Me too."

He shifted his head, intending to kiss her, but she pushed against his chest.

"Hold on, Dr. Eager Beaver. I'm dying to feel those hot lips of yours on mine, but give me your word that you'll stop at just one kiss and you won't hoist me onto this counter and do all sorts of depraved things to me."

"Why not?"

"Oh, don't look butt hurt. I need *your* promise to stop because I know once I get in that lust-addled state, I'll say yes to anything."

"And that's bad…?"

"Not normally. We will get down and dirty until we're both hoarse and half dead in a sex coma. But first I need to feed you." She kissed the inside of his wrist. "You've subsisted on coffee and beef jerky for two days. You need real food to fuel up. It'd be a shame if this amazing body would peter out at the magic moment, wouldn't it?"

"Are you questioning my stamina, Miss Gradsky?" His fingers slipped down to cup the back of her neck. "The first round might be lightning fast. But I promise you rounds two, three, four, and five won't be."

Holy shit. He planned to fuck her five times?

Yes, please.

Then Liam took her mouth like a conquering hero, caging her body with his, gripping the nape of her neck to keep her head where he wanted it, gifting her with a head-swimming kiss that satisfied any qualms about how well the man used his lips and tongue.

She was embarrassingly breathless—and wet—when he released her with a nuzzle below her ear.

He stepped back and smiled. "Only one kiss, as requested."

"Thank you. Now park it on the other side of the breakfast bar." She propped her hand on her hip and challenged, "Or do I have to banish you because you're the type of guy who'll freak out when I rummage in your fridge and make a huge mess on the counters and the stove?"

A horrified look crossed his face.

"I thought so." She pointed at the living room. "Go. And no smoking the good stuff while I'm slaving away."

"Why are you bossing me around in my own kitchen?"

"Because I'll let you boss me around in your bedroom later."

He flashed a wicked grin. "Excellent trade-off."

Stirling whipped up veggie omelets with cream cheese and capers, and a pile of toast.

Liam ate slowly, despite how hungry he must've been.

"You have great manners. Not that I'm surprised," she added.

"Thank you. My gramma would've been happy to hear that her nagging all those years hadn't been for naught."

Then he didn't say anything else.

She sighed. "You're going to make me ask, aren't you?"

"Ask what?"

"Why your grandma would be proud and not your mother."

Liam wiped his mouth with a napkin and then knocked back the last of his coffee. "Because my gramma raised me. My mother ditched me with her when I was five."

"Oh. Well, I can skip the question about whether you have any siblings and go straight to the others I have."

"Stirling—"

"Uh-uh. I blathered on about my life history; it's only fair that I hear yours."

"No, you shared your work history and how it related to you getting into the cannabis industry. You didn't talk at all of your childhood."

"Fine." She snatched his last piece of toast. "I've heard some of your work history, so tell me how a brilliant man with a doctorate in microbiology opted to specialize in cannabis."

He wrinkled his brow. "You really want to do this now?"

"Why not? Is there somewhere else you need to be?"

No response.

Great, he'd reverted to Dr. Aloof. Stirling picked up the dishes and headed to the sink. "That's right. You have unicycling club tonight. Or is this the night you're rounding up the posse to track Bigfoot? I can't keep your hobbies straight." She squirted soap into the stream of hot water and reached for the sponge.

A tattooed hand shut off the water. Then warm, strong arms encircled her. He rested his chin on the top of her head. "I suck at this stuff, Stirling. Like epic-level suck. Some events in my past are embarrassing."

"Liam, everyone has embarrassing moments in their past they'd rather forget. That's not what I asked you to share with me."

His breath fanned across the top of her head. "What if they're one and the same?"

"Meaning what?"

"Meaning…getting busted for possession at age seventeen is also why I pushed myself to get through college, with an eye on earning a doctorate so I could focus my plant-science research solely on cannabis, so I could help people like my gramma." His arms slipped free and she heard him walk away.

Since Liam needed to cool down or nut up before they resumed the conversation, Stirling took her time washing the dishes and cleaning the kitchen. Then she checked her phone for messages, looked at cute pictures of kittens on Instagram, and drank three cups of coffee.

Forty minutes later and Liam still hadn't shown his face.

All right, he wasn't ready to let her in—which seemed a more positive way of phrasing it than he'd shut her out—so she'd go home and chalk this up to a bad idea.

After folding the flannel shirt and setting it on the counter, she grabbed her satchel. As she passed through the hall to the entryway, she didn't bother to peek into the living room to see if Dr. Detached had conked out on the couch.

It was just her luck that she lost her balance as she slipped on her cowgirl boot, falling sideways into the coat tree, knocking it over with a spectacular crash.

So much for her stealth exit.

Liam raced around the corner. "Stirling? Are you…"

"Leaving? Yes. Get some rest, Dr. Argent. I'll see you at work tomorrow."

His eyes narrowed. "You're pissed off at me."

"What makes you think that?"

"You called me Dr. Argent."

"It *is* your name, as you've repeatedly reminded me over the past ten months. Anyway, I'm not pissed off because you don't want to discuss your past with me. It's your choice. I'm not the type to nag or beg. But relationships require a level of trust from both parties, otherwise it's superficial. I've had enough of that, so I'll pass if that's all you're prepared to offer me." She bent down to retrieve her boot….and found herself airborne with Liam's shoulder in her stomach as he carried her in a fireman's hold into the living room.

Stirling was so stunned by his caveman behavior she couldn't speak.

Liam laid her on the couch and stretched out on top of her, preventing her escape.

The smart man had pinned her legs so she couldn't knee him in the balls, either.

So she glared at him. She'd said her piece; in fact, she'd probably said far too much.

"Did you mean it?" he demanded.

"Mean what? Mean to leave? Yes."

"No. Did you mean it that we're in a relationship?"

The vulnerability in his eyes just...slayed her. "The pranks, the bickering, the one-upmanship... We've been in a relationship since day one, Dr. Dumbass. An adversarial relationship, sort of fucked-up, to be honest. But in that time... Have I permeated your thoughts to the point you aren't sure if you want to strangle me or if you want to fuck me? Do you have entire conversations in your head about what clever remarks you'll toss off the next time you run into me? Or maybe you *plan* to cross my path just so we can have a snarky back and forth? Does your heart race when you see me? Do you imagine shutting my smart mouth with a steamy kiss? Do you fantasize about storming into my office, locking the door, bending me over my desk, fucking me in silence until we both explode, and then leaving without saying a word?"

"Yes."

"Yes to what?"

"Yes to all of it."

That's when she noticed he wasn't wearing his glasses. He looked less haughty. Less closed off. But still so sexy she couldn't catch her breath.

Or maybe you can't breathe because the man is squishing you.

But Stirling wasn't about to complain.

"You believe that us fighting, playing practical jokes, and acting like mortal enemies has been some kind of prolonged foreplay?"

She snorted. "Dude. It's *still* foreplay since we haven't fucked."

"*Yet.*" Liam kissed her. Not with hunger but with sweet seduction. Soft, teasing nibbles, followed by the slick slide of his lips. Tasting her. Tormenting her. Finally, he slowed the sensual assault on her mouth.

"Please tell me that kiss was the last bout of foreplay before you fuck me mindless."

He chuckled and planted a lingering smooch on her lips. "No. That was a *thank you for voicing everything I couldn't* kiss." Another smooch. "A *you understand me and aren't running away yelling* freak *at me* kiss." A longer press of his lips. "An *I'm ready to talk honestly about my past* kiss..." His eyes gleamed. "But let's have a couple of hits first."

Stirling laughed. "Good plan. As long as there's hair-pulling fucking afterward."

"You truly are the perfect woman, Stirling Gradsky." He pushed back and stood.

She scooted around into a sitting position.

He looked over his shoulder at her after he pulled out his weed box.

"Where's my shirt?"

"On the counter. Why? Did you think I stole it?"

"No. I liked seeing you wear it. Never had anyone do that before."

That he'd admitted such a sweet sentiment... She felt oddly honored.

Like before, Liam arranged the cannabis essentials in a precise row. Stirling noticed he'd pulled out a vaporizer pen—one that used concentrated oil instead of bud or wax.

He caught her watching him. "Don't know if I can deal with any more smoke today."

"Understood. What tasty concoction are you creating for us?"

"Just a mix of oils I've found that don't gum up in this thing."

"Cool. That's probably why I don't mess with oils. I had a pen like that for buds."

"We all have our likes and dislikes." He placed the mouthpiece on.

"What is your dislike?"

"Dabbing."

"Why?"

"Using a blowtorch to vaporize concentrates is a complicated and dangerous process when there are so many other options. Plus, I get way high, way too fast." He handed her the vape pen first.

The taste remained citrusy smooth, even through her exhale. "I like that."

Liam indulged in a huge hit and passed the pen back. "I've found two tokes to be the perfect ratio."

"I'll stick with one."

After he finished his second hit, he set the pen next to his eyeglasses on the table. Then he stretched out on the couch, tugging her down with him so the side of her face rested on his chest. "Are you comfortable?"

She tried not to let it bother her that he'd chosen this position so he wouldn't have to look her in the eye when he talked of his past. Turning her hips, she threw her leg over his. "Now I am."

"Good." Liam began lightly dragging his fingertips up and down her arm. He brushed one soft, warm kiss up high on her forehead before he spoke. "I don't remember my mother at all. She ditched me at her mom's when I was five. My earliest memory was sitting at Gramma's kitchen table, eating a deviled ham sandwich. It's still my comfort food. Anyway, I attended public school until I was twelve. After taking a standardized test, my teacher, the school counselor, and the principal called Gramma and me in for a meeting."

"Let me guess. Your scores were off the chart."

He chuckled. "The highest they'd ever seen. Apparently the highest for my grade level in the entire state. They urged Gramma to enroll me in a private school for the academically gifted. Keep in mind that my sixty-five-year-old gramma worked as a daytime janitor. We barely scraped by. There was no way she could afford private school. But the school counselor was determined to find the tuition. And she did. Scholarships up the wazoo. We needed to 'only' come up with an extra two hundred dollars."

"For the entire year?"

"No. Two hundred dollars per month. So Gramma switched to the nighttime janitorial crew since it paid more. I enrolled in private school that fall. I hated the uniforms, hated the hierarchy, hated being the skinny poor kid. It didn't help that I academically outpaced my fellow students so they had an excuse to make my life hell. Whenever Gramma asked about school, I lied and swore it was awesome. On an academic level it was challenging. That part I loved. The social aspect? A nightmare. One thing I hadn't known? Working the night shift paid more because there was more work to do. It wore my grandmother down. She already had arthritis and she developed chronic pain syndrome. Her insurance wouldn't cover high-priced pain meds, so she sucked it up and suffered." His fingers stopped moving on her arm. "That's what I hated most of all. She'd given up so much to raise me. It killed me to see her curled into a ball in her bed because her body hurt so badly. I felt helpless and guilty and told her I'd go back to public school, but she refused to consider it."

"How old were you?"

"At that time...fifteen."

"Did you have anyone to talk to?"

"I'd made one friend—Dougie—we social outcasts stuck together. He'd landed in private school after being expelled from public school for smoking pot. So I confided in him. He suggested I get a nighttime job to help out financially. He also mentioned that marijuana had medicinal properties and gave me a joint. Of course, I balked. Gramma wouldn't consider getting high, right? But one day the pain was so bad I bucked up and asked her if it would help."

Stirling felt him swallow.

"After I convinced her I wasn't doing drugs—I'd done research on cannabis to find a way to help her—she finally tried it. It eased her pain, but she didn't like the smoking part. I tracked down a water vapor heavy bong, hoping it delivered on the promise of less smoke but equal medical benefits."

"What about edibles?"

"Edibles…inconsistent information at that time. It was more of a joke. 'Hey, you want my Aunt Ginny's recipe for pot brownies?'"

Stirling snickered. "And she'd probably have to eat an entire pan of them."

"Exactly. Since she didn't have another option, she kept lighting up."

"Dougie was your dealer?"

"No. At first he'd supplied me out of his own stash. When I learned how much Gramma needed and how much it cost, Dougie set me up with a dealer."

"Wait… Dougie. Why is that name familiar?"

"Because he's the cannabis specialist who helped me deal with the plants Friday night. I've never met anyone who knows more than he does."

"You're still friends with him?"

"We kept in touch over the years. He's a brilliant guy, but the crazy kind of brilliant."

"Like attracts like. He's a perfect friend for you," she teased.

Liam lightly tapped her ass.

"What does he do for a living?"

"He won't admit to it, but I'd lay odds he's a hacker."

"Wow. He's not in the cannabis industry?"

"He grows his own. When we were teens he turned his closet into a grow house."

"Enterprising."

"Selfish with his product, but not his knowledge. So when I discovered cannabis could be ingested in pill form, he helped me learn how to make them. We screwed up a bunch of times before we got the viscosity right."

"Were pills easier for your grandma?"

"Much. I kept a notebook detailing…well, everything. Especially how her body responded. Sometimes she got a head high and fell asleep. Other times she'd get an energetic full-body boost. But it worked. There wasn't a chance she could OD, like with oxy. Pharmaceutical companies manufacture drugs full of dangerous and deadly chemicals. But cannabis, which is natural and nonaddictive, is illegal. Makes no sense on any level."

"Preaching to the choir, Liam."

He sighed. "I know." His hand had drifted to her arm. The rough tips of his fingers trailed from the ball of her shoulder to the inside of her wrist.

"Your grandma didn't have a problem sending her teenaged grandson out onto the streets of Denver to buy weed for her?"

"She had a serious issue with it. So I lied. I told her I was buying from Dougie, but she couldn't ever let on that she knew."

"Sneaky."

"Not sneaky enough."

She propped her chin on his chest and looked at him. "What happened?"

"I started working for my dealer. Partially because he gave me a discount on my biweekly purchase. Partially because it paid more than bussing tables and it allowed me more free time to apply for college scholarships and grants."

"When you mean working for...?"

"I delivered packages a couple times a week. I had no idea what was in them—I didn't *want* to know. But given what he did for a living... It was obvious. Anyway, I'd been his 'errand' boy for about a year. That day's delivery was to a fitness club. I had the locker number and the combination memorized. But evidently a skinny, nerdy-looking kid with glasses roused suspicion among the body builders, so the front desk manager detained me. The cops came, searched my backpack, and found the unmarked package."

"What did they find when they opened it?"

"Baggies of pills. Hash. Mushrooms. I didn't have to feign shock because I *was* shocked. They cuffed me and dragged me to juvenile. I couldn't get ahold of my gramma so the cops brought in a woman from social services. That allowed them to start grilling me. Even when I hoped it never happened, getting caught had always been a possibility, so I had a cover story."

"Which was?"

"A big body builder dude stopped me at the end of the block and said he wanted to play a joke on his buddy. Said he'd pay me twenty bucks to take a package into the locker room, write 'John' on the outside, and leave it in an empty locker. The cops didn't believe me and kept asking the same questions over and over. My answers never wavered. So they decided to book me for possession, figuring I'd crack when faced with jail time." He fidgeted beneath her. "I cried. In fucking juvie. I was terrified to spend even one night in there, wearing inmate orange."

"Did anything bad happen?"

"No. The other kids ignored me. The next morning I had an appearance in juvenile court and Gramma was there so they released me. The cops testified, calling my explanation a 'total fabrication'. The front desk manager admitted they had several members named John."

"Ah, the first seeds of doubt."

He yawned. "I had two 'character' witnesses. The school counselor who helped me get into private school and my physics teacher. They touted my academics, my flawless disciplinary record, and my helpful nature. Neither of them had trouble believing I'd do a favor for a stranger. With no prior history of arrests, the judge dismissed the charges."

"So nothing went on your permanent record."

"Nope." He stretched and rested his forearm across his eyes. "That's the benefit of a dealer using underage couriers."

"Did he know you'd gotten caught?"

"Of course. He cut me loose. But for not ratting him out, he left me five hundred grams of weed under my pillow."

"Over a pound? Seriously?"

"Mmm-hmm."

"What did your grandma say about your stint in juvie?"

"She asked if I was dealing for Dougie." Another jaw-cracking yawn. "I didn't have to lie to her about that."

Stirling nestled into his chest. "Thanks for telling me."

"You're welcome. But it's still embarrassing," he mumbled.

"During my teen years I didn't hang around with kids who bragged about juvie like it was a private club. Bad boys... I never understood the attraction. Not that they were attracted to me, a girl with braces and acne, not to mention my hard line of what was right and what was wrong. No gray areas in my world. My friends were like me—focused on academics and what came after high school. My sister wasn't. At the time she made me feel like a loser for not running wild like she did.

Looking back, I was too afraid acting tough and reckless wouldn't make a difference in how other kids my age saw me. And looking like you were trying too hard to be cool was worse than just accepting that you weren't and didn't fit in, know what I mean?"

No answer.

His breathing had evened out, meaning he'd fallen asleep.

Stupid karma.

"Fine. I deserve this. But is the 'payback's a bitch' smirk necessary, Dr. Dozed Off?"

No response.

"I'm really glad I didn't take that second hit."

She listened to his slow and steady heartbeat. It'd been a rough couple of days and he needed sleep more than sex. She disentangled from him and he didn't move.

After she covered him with that butt-ugly crocheted afghan, she perched on the edge of the couch and watched him sleep. "Are we ever gonna get this right?"

Stirling grabbed her stuff—including his flannel shirt—and went home.

Chapter Eight

Chaos ruled at High Society on Monday morning.

With one half of the stage-one grow house padlocked on the outside and hermetically sealed on the inside, employees were justifiably spooked.

Liam had taken delivery of the extraction machine and was waiting for the contractors to arrive, when Kiki, the consultant who handled paperwork for the various revenue and enforcement agencies, showed up in terrorize mode. Not only hadn't they called her when the MED agents were onsite, with Macon out of the country for an indeterminate amount of time, she'd have to deal with Stirling.

He watched Kiki barrel into Stirling's office—but she only got as far as Stirling's assistant Shanna's desk. So as Kiki paced and texted on her phone, Liam leaned in the doorway, figuring he should stick around in case Stirling needed moral support.

Or maybe you want to see Stirling shift into ass-kicking mode because it's highly entertaining… Especially when you're not on the receiving end.

Shanna crossed over to Stirling's office and opened the door. "Miss Gradsky will see you now."

"About goddamned time." Kiki stormed in and Shanna left the door open so Liam could follow her.

Stirling flicked a quick look at him but her expression didn't change. "Kiki. Won't you have a seat?"

"No." She slammed her hands on the desk and loomed over Stirling. "I want to know what is going on here *right now*. First, there was an infestation that required the MED onsite for hours as the affected plants were destroyed and no one contacted me. Then I find out there's an industrial extraction machine going in? And once again, no one told me about this development or asked about the dozens of hours that will be added to my workload."

Stirling tapped her pen on her desk blotter and studied Kiki coolly. "Is that all?"

"Is that all?" Kiki exploded. "Don't you think that is enough?"

Stirling rolled her office chair back and stood. Then she mimicked Kiki's pose, angling her body across the desk until they were face to face. "With all due respect, Kiki, I *own* this business. I don't answer to you. I certainly don't need your permission to purchase equipment for my business."

Liam did a mental fist pump.

"Dr. Argent handled the situation with MED. He told me about the outbreak as soon as it was discovered and the measures he'd taken to contain it. I was here Sunday when the authorities were onsite. Besides Dr. Argent, I was the only person required to be here. What I didn't want to have happen is exactly what happened when you came storming in here like an ill wind, throwing out accusations and rattling my employees."

Kiki's back snapped straight. "I only—"

Stirling held up her hand. "You acted as if you have more power here than you really do. While Macon and I appreciate the work you've done for our company in the past, if you believe the decision we made together last week will create more work than you're willing to take on, I'd completely understand if you felt the need to turn in your resignation."

Damn. Miss Gradsky was sneaky good. It gave him a feeling of…not pride, but…

Lust.

Beautiful, brilliant, belligerent… The woman had massive balls.

When a dude pisses me off I'm gonna tell him to woman up and grow a goddamn uterus. Balls are for pussies.

Thankfully he'd perfected his poker face or he might've started laughing.

"Wait. I didn't say I wanted to quit."

Watching Kiki backtrack wasn't nearly as interesting as seeing the class and grace that Stirling used to handle her.

Oh. And hand Kiki her ass.

The rest of the conversation lasted about four minutes.

He stepped aside, allowing Kiki to exit. When he grabbed the handle to close the door, Shanna, the office assistant from hell, blocked the door open with her body.

"Nice try, Dr. Argent. But I doubt Miss Gradsky wants to be stuck in here with you."

Want to bet?

"And the cleaning service charges extra to remove blood from the walls and carpet," she added.

"It's all right, Shanna. Liam and I have a few boring matters to discuss in private."

Boring? Ouch.

Shanna had frozen in the threshold with her mouth hanging open.

He said, "Hold her calls," and shut the door in Shanna's face.

And locked it.

When he turned around, Stirling was still standing. "Well, if it isn't Rip Van Winkle."

"Nice to see you too, Sleeping Beauty." He stopped behind the visitor's chair in front of her desk. "I'm sorry for falling asleep last night."

She shrugged. "Now we're even."

"Are we? Remember what transpired in *my* office the day after you crashed at my place?" He began to stalk her. And she played the prey so well; she started backing up.

"You kissed me."

"So for it to be truly even between us, Miss Gradsky...?"

"Then you'd better come here, Dr. Hottie, and pucker up."

Liam kept walking forward until he'd pinned her against the wall.

Then Stirling's mouth was on his in a carnal kiss. She jammed one hand in his hair and the other gripped his lapel. She poured every bit of hunger and sexual frustration into him. Grinding her hot body into his. Making sexy noises as she sucked on his tongue and pulled his hair.

Good thing he'd locked his knees. And the door.

When she finally released his mouth she said, "We really shouldn't be doing this."

He laughed against her lips and said, "No we shouldn't," initiating another ravenous kiss.

She dug her nails into his scalp trying to keep him in place as he slid his lips up her jawline. "Getting involved with a coworker is a bad idea," she panted in his ear.

"Very bad," he said, sucking on the pulse point in her throat.

"It never works out," she murmured, arching back, offering him full access.

"Never," he repeated. With his hands squeezing her ass, he hoisted her higher against the wall. He brushed butterfly soft kisses over the shell of her ear. "Do you want me to stop?"

She said, "Don't you dare," and returned his lips to hers by hooking her arm around his neck.

The heat between them blazed.

Stirling whimpered softly when he slowed the kiss down.

Liam forced himself to take a break while his big head retained control of his body, before his brain surrendered that control to his dick. He exhaled a breath and rested his forehead on her shoulder.

"Why the big sigh, big guy?"

"I don't want this to be just dirty talk between us."

"I thought we established that last night," she said carefully.

"And we established that on Friday, too."

"Oh. Right. Now I get what you're saying."

"The missed sexy time opportunities have gnawed at me since I woke up alone this morning. Even when I know it's ridiculous, because it's only been three days since the massive shift in our attitudes toward each other. Yet it feels—"

"Like you've been waiting to get naked with me for a lot longer," she finished.

Liam lifted his head and looked at her. "You feel it too."

"Of course I do. We've known each other ten months, Liam. We didn't like each other. Or at least pretended not to like each other so it masked our mutual attraction. We certainly didn't take the time to get to know each other outside of work."

"Have you had a life outside of work in the past year?"

Stirling blinked those beautiful blue eyes at him. "No. There's so damn much to do around here. So much more that I *want* to do. Even if I'm onsite fourteen hours a day, seven days a week, it isn't enough."

"Exactly." He pushed an errant dreadlock over her shoulder. "Our work selves *are* who we are. There's no mystery to me, Stirling. It's embarrassing to admit I've always been this..."

"Work obsessed?"

"Yes. I recognized that common element in you before we dropped the attitudes and started communicating on a different level."

Smiling, she pressed a soft kiss to his chin. "I prefer this more intimate manner of communication anyway. I was running low on prank ideas."

Liam stared at her, wondering if she'd taken their pranks at face value. When to him they'd always been so much more.

"Why so serious all of a sudden, Dr. Sad Eyes?"

"Just...hypothesizing."

She rolled her eyes. "Scientists."

"Tell me five personal things you learned about me during our prank wars."

"Why?"

"So, suspicious, Miss Gradsky." He planted a quick kiss on her mouth. "I need to prove a theory."

"If I do it, you have to do it too."

"Of course." *And I intend to win this "What I Like About You" face-off.*

"You listen to blues music in your lab when things are going well and no music when you're frustrated."

"Excellent observation. That's one."

"You whistle in the break room if you're by yourself."

His face heated.

Stirling laughed. "It's cute. And it's cute how you blush."

Cute. Great. "That's two."

"You enjoy talking to Hip in the drying room. You two can blather on about nuances of varieties for hours. The first time I ever heard you laugh you were shooting the shit with him. If Hip gets behind, you help him. You even let him tell you what to do, which annoyed the piss out of me."

"Hip is a West Coast guy. He knows his weed. You're up to three."

"You have the longest eyelashes I've ever seen. Your eyes are a silvery light gray, unless you're angry and then they darken to pewter."

"While I appreciate the compliment, that's not a valid answer. Another personal example, not a physical attribute."

"Fine. You wear the same watch every day." She tapped the face of it. "Four months ago...you showed up on a Tuesday morning, sans watch. You were so bad tempered, I worried if you'd lost it, you'd blame me for taking it. Then two weeks later, the trusty watch was back on your wrist."

"Gramma gave me that watch for college graduation. It quit

working and the repair guy wasn't sure he could fix it. But he did."

"Luckily for all of us."

"Last one."

Stirling's fingers slid up the back of his neck and she scraped her nails against his scalp. A groan escaped. Damn. That felt good. "This super trendy haircut looks awesome on you. Total dick move on my part to leave the 'What Your Haircut Says About You' article in your lab along with a pair of scissors."

He chuckled. "I get it. Jumanji, budtender supreme, rocks the man bun. I didn't. I did need a haircut. Flattery won't change the fact that answer is invalid, so try again."

She stared at him so long he began to sweat whatever answer she was wrestling with.

"Are you stumped?"

"No, I could give a dozen more examples. But the one that's most telling about you, Dr. Argent, is that you take out the trash every night. It started the first month we opened and Shanna got accosted by the homeless guys hanging out by the Dumpster. You saw how upset she was. The very next day Macon handed down an edict that no one was to go out there alone and at the end of shift, all trash should be left in the back entryway. The employees assume the cleaning service handles disposing of it. Sometimes they do. But most of the time, it's you."

"I had no idea you noticed that, Stirling."

She fiddled with the collar of his lab coat. "That means if we do this, it wouldn't just be a fuck that we could blame on elevated emotions. It wouldn't be an 'oops, we were high' excuse either."

"That's what I'm saying." He framed her face in his hands. "I want you so fucking bad that I locked the goddamned door on the off chance I'd get to bend you over your desk."

She gave him a coy smile. "Given how things have gone for us in the past three days... That's just begging the universe for an untimely interruption, isn't it?"

"Undoubtedly. Especially when you consider you called me *Liam* in front of your assistant, and not Dr. Argent, Dr. Asshat, or any of your other colorful nicknames for me."

"Shit. I did call you Liam, all friendly-like, when as far as she—or anyone else who works here believes—we're still in deep dislike of each other." Stirling squirmed to be let go. "I'm surprised Shanna's gone this long without interrupting." She started to walk past him but he caught her arm.

"Will you tell her that we're…?"

"Currently not fucking? I'm pretty sure she already knows."

It surprised him this conversation made her nervous. Or perhaps the idea of telling other people about them brought out her flippancy.

"Look. I want to keep what happens between us…private, okay?" Stirling said.

"Meaning we resume bickering and trying to one-up each other during working hours?"

She blew out a breath. "No. We're beyond that. But all joking aside, we've both been burned by relationships with coworkers. Neither of us needs to have our professionalism questioned."

He furrowed his brow.

"What?"

"So fucking you over your desk isn't a possibility?"

Stirling laughed when she realized he was joking. "Not today."

But the truth was he was only half-joking. "Seems a shame to put the condoms I stashed in my lab coat pocket back into the box."

"You don't have condoms in your pocket," she scoffed.

"You sure?" Liam fought a smile when he challenged, "Maybe you should find out for yourself."

"You probably put a joy buzzer in your pocket."

"I'd prefer you stuck your hand down my pants and wrapped your fingers around my joy *stick*," he said and stole a kiss. "Don't be scared."

"Scared? As if." Stirling locked her gaze to his, inching her hand down the center of his body. "Did you dress left or right today?" She smirked. "I mean, left pocket or right pocket?"

Ridiculous how fast his heart raced just from her touch. "Left."

She switched the angle of her hand and slipped it into his pocket. Shifting his lab coat to the right, she squeezed his hard-on once, then her hand exited his pocket holding a fistful of condoms. Amusement danced in her eyes. "Only ten, Dr. *Ardent?*"

He shrugged. "I thought twenty might be overkill."

"Maybe. Since we've yet to use even one."

"Don't pout." Liam snagged the strip out of her hands. "How about this? I'll put these back…except for this one."

"Why is it special?"

Watching her face, he ripped the top packet off with his teeth and bent down to nuzzle her cleavage, tucking the condom into her bra cup.

He softly kissed a line up her chest to her mouth, pausing to show her the heat in his eyes. "Let me know when you're ready to use it. The ball—or maybe I should say my balls—are in your court." He shoved the long strip back in his pocket and walked away.

Chapter Nine

Why would Liam put the decision for when they became lovers solely in her hands?

Because he didn't care one way or the other?

No. He'd shown up in her office with condoms. He wasn't exactly "whatever" about them getting it on.

Maybe you should stop worrying about funny business and get back to running your business.

Good plan.

Stirling lasted three hours—most of which she'd spent on the phone—before she decided to check on the installation of their newest piece of equipment.

The designated space housing the new machine was across the hallway from the lab. The door was open and she heard *clank, clank, clank*, then "Motherfuck!"

"Is everything all right?" she called through the door.

Liam's face appeared on the left side of the CO_2 tank. "Macon may've gotten a great deal on this, but it should've been industrially cleaned before they sold it."

"It's not defective?" she said with alarm.

"Not that I can tell. Just dirty. When the technicians arrive they'll hear it from me. There's no excuse for poor maintenance of lab equipment." Liam's head disappeared for a moment and then he shuffled toward her.

Stirling couldn't believe her eyes. Dr. Argent's pristine white lab coat? Filthy. Grease stains were smeared down the front as if he'd actually used it as a towel.

He said "What?" a little tersely.

"Dude. A truckload of Tide bleach pens won't do the trick on those stains."

"As I'm aware."

When she looked at his face, she couldn't help but break out in laughter.

"Find my dishevelment amusing?"

"I wouldn't say…amusing."

"What would you say?"

"Surprising. I've never seen you less than perfectly put together. You look like one of those hot-rod mechanics, dirt on your face, smears of grease on your clothes, oil on your rough, knuckled hands. Your tattoos peeking out just adds that rugged-around-the-edges hotness."

Liam stalked her for the second time today. Her back hit the wall and those big, dirty hands were right next to her head. "Is that what turns you on? A guy with workingman's hands?" He put his mouth close to her ear. "Do you imagine your man coming home from an honest day's labor, pulling a cold beer out of the fridge, and seeking you out before he changes out of his stained work clothes?"

He brushed a kiss below her earlobe, eliciting her shiver.

"When this blue-collar fantasy man sees his sexy-as-fuck woman wearing a tight skirt that molds your perfect ass, and you turn around, your hard nipples taunting him under your sheer white blouse, does he drain his beer in one long drink, never taking his eyes off of you? Do his work boots thump against the floor, matching the fast beat of your heart, as he comes closer and pins you against the wall?"

Her heart rate went wild.

"Does he put those big, dirty hands on your tits and capture your mouth in a brutal kiss? As he's touching you everywhere, kissing you, rubbing his body on yours, determined to take what's his…" Liam's lips moved to her neck, placing a line of kisses to the center of her chest. "Do you even care that he's left grease stains on your chest, your ass, your thighs, and your throat? Or do you wear those dirty marks with pride?"

"Liam—"

"Answer me," he demanded, his mouth against her throat.

"No, I don't care."

"Why not?"

She swallowed the ball of lust in her throat. "To feel—to see—firsthand that kind of sexual need directed at me, knowing I brought it out in him? Knowing I'm what he desires above all else in that moment in time? That I'm the one who can satisfy him? That's heady stuff."

Liam allowed enough space between them to gaze into her eyes.

His expression convinced her to confess, "Especially when I've never had that."

A beat passed and he said, "You do now."

Oh. Fuck.

Then he retreated. "I'll put a pin in that fantasy for now."

"What? You're just..." *Leaving me here all wet and horny?*

"Ushering you back to work? Yes." A cocky smile curled his lips. "We're acting professional, keeping this a secret between us, not risking our reputations...*blah, blah, blah*... Sound familiar?"

Stirling blushed. She *had* said that. Fuck. *Why* had she said that?

"I'm following your lead, Miss Gradsky."

That cleared her lusty thoughts. "And why is that? Why leave the decision about our first sexy time up to me?"

"Because you have more doubts about this than I do."

"Not true, Dr. Delusional. You asked me to help prove your theory. I shared five observations about you. Instead of participating, you handed me a condom and bailed. Which indicates that you couldn't come up with *one* thing you learned about me during prankfest, to say nothing of five."

"Wrong."

"Prove it."

The muscle in his jaw flexed like he was gritting his teeth. "One. You have half a dozen pairs of cowgirl boots, but when you have an important meeting and need an extra boost of confidence, you wear your beat-up brown leather boots, because you consider them lucky."

Dammit.

"Two. You keep a bag of cat food behind the seat in your monster truck to feed the strays by the fence."

Her mouth dropped open. "How do you know that?"

"I noticed the bag when I filled your truck cab with 'I Love Nick Jonas' balloons."

"The joke was on you that time, because I'm a *Joe* Jonas fan." She sighed. "That guy is fucking fine." Actually...when she thought about it... There was a resemblance between Joe and Liam.

"Three," he continued tersely, "you won't drink citrus-based sodas, even if 7Up is the only kind left in the vending machine. But you love Diet Mountain Dew."

"Everyone who works here knows that, so number four needs to knock my socks off."

"You brush your teeth at work at least twice a day. You have a special pink plastic case you tuck in your purse." He tipped his head closer and licked the seam of her lips. "As a man who's had my tongue in this delectable mouth, I thank you for the attention to oral hygiene. I could kiss you for hours."

Stirling forced herself to ignore the sexy growling noise he made, even when her pulse sped up. "Finish it. Number five."

"I noticed you in Macon's office the first time I met him. When he excused himself to take a call, I wandered to the shelf behind his desk and saw a picture of him standing next to the most beautiful woman I'd ever seen. Her smile lit up the picture, so I couldn't fathom how formidable that smile would be in real life. The casual way she leaned into Macon, her dreadlocks a complete contradiction to the business suit he wore, showed a woman confident with who she is." His gaze encompassed her entire face. "I'd never envied a man as much as I did Macon in that moment."

The intensity in his eyes made simply breathing difficult.

"When Macon returned and saw me holding the picture, I told him his girlfriend was stunning. He laughed and said, 'That's my little sister.' And he said nothing else. Not that if I agreed to work for High Society, I'd see your mesmerizing smile every goddamned day. Not that we'd detest each other on sight. Not that we were exactly alike and we'd immediately become BFFs. Not that we'd develop an intimate connection through crazy, stupid pranks." He put his mouth on her ear. "And most definitely not that you and I would throw enough sexual sparks off each other to power all the lights in the grow house."

"Liam."

"I've gotten more satisfaction from fighting with you the past ten months than I've *ever* gotten from fucking any woman."

"Okay, you win," she said in a breathless rush.

"I'd say we're both winners."

In the silence she heard the heels clicking down the hallway stop outside the door.

Shanna called, "Dr. Argent?" through the door.

"Yes?"

"Have you seen Stirling?"

"She's right here."

Stirling stepped around Liam. "Hey, Shan, what's up?"

Her confused gaze winged between them. "Some of the employees are freaked out about all that's gone on, so you need to settle them down."

"Don't we have weed that'll take care of that better than I can?"

Liam laughed behind her.

"Oh, stuff it," she said over her shoulder. "It's not funny."

He kept laughing. "Yes, Stirling, it is."

"Whatever. Quit playing with your tool and double check when the contractors are supposed to arrive."

"As you wish."

Shannon's jaw nearly dragged on the floor as she tried to keep up with Stirling hustling down the hallway.

Before they entered the back room—technically the drying room, the trimming room, and the vault where the saleable "finished" weed was stored—Stirling faced her assistant. "Why is everyone freaked out?"

"Because they're afraid the business is going under."

Of all the... She counted to ten. "What gave them that impression?"

"Oh, I don't know. Grow stage one was padlocked by the MED, and Macon isn't around after he had meetings with you and Dr. Argent two days in a row last week."

"That's it? Macon is rarely around." She'd be really happy if he became a silent partner.

"No, that's not it." Shanna shuffled her feet. "You and Dr. Argent aren't arguing and acting like Dwight and Jim on *The Office.* The employees are afraid you're getting along because the business is folding."

Talk about stoner paranoia. "The business is fine. My brother insisted Liam—Dr. Argent—and I work together on getting the extraction equipment viable as soon as possible."

"That's it?"

"Yes." Stirling slid her keycard through the reader and waited for the green light.

Once the door opened that distinctive cannabis scent wafted out.

The door to the drying room was at the end of a short hallway. She stepped inside and her gaze swept the ceiling. Cotton clotheslines were strung from one end of the room to the other. Each plant hung upside down with the RFID still attached.

Hip, the post-harvest manager, aka the "cannabis sommelier," bounded over. "Hey, boss lady. What's up?"

"Typical Monday shit." Stirling's gaze locked onto the vault. She still couldn't wrap her head around the fact that hundreds of thousands of dollars' worth of product finished the drying process in garbage bags. Then she looked back at Hip. "Just giving you a heads' up. We're enacting some changes—all good ones, I promise. I'll make a formal announcement and write up protocol, but all of these leaves and shit pieces that drop during drying? They'll need to be picked up and screened for the extraction machine."

"You got it."

"The next harvest is in two weeks?"

He nodded. "We'll be ready. We're sitting good on stock of the popular kinds. But tell Jumanji we've got an extra bag of OG Kush to run as a happy hour special this week."

"How much extra?"

"Ten pounds." Hip shook his head. "Man, Louie was a fuck-up. Or he planned to rip you off. That much bud shouldn't have been where I found it. I'm glad he's gone."

Employee turnover was higher than normal in this business. "You're sure it's marked recreational and not medicinal?"

"Positive."

"Awesome. Split it in half. Mark one of the bags for me. We'll need to run premium buds through the extractor after we're familiar with the machine."

"Will do."

"Thanks, Hip."

The door between the drying room and trimming area required another keycard entry. Since trimmers weren't employees, but independent contractors, they had limited access behind the scenes.

Josie, a carrot-topped, freckle-faced waif with a photographic memory, managed the trimming and packaging room. She froze when Stirling entered. "Fuck. It's true. We're closing."

"No, we're not closing. We're making some changes but none of them are bad."

Her eyes narrowed. "Who's we?"

"Me mostly. But Dr. Argent will be working outside of his lab. So cooperate with him, yeah?"

"No problemo."

Stirling relayed the new instructions for gathering the trim that didn't make the final cuts. "Any questions?"

"You want the super trash too? Stems, etc.?"

"Yeah. Why?"

"That's what I'm asking. Trash parts are *trash* for a reason. What do you think you're gonna get out of it?"

"We won't know unless we experiment with the low end as well as the high end. Dr. Argent will determine a baseline and we'll go from there."

"Oh. That makes sense. Thanks for explaining everything. I know you didn't have to." Josie adjusted her headband. "I have a buddy who works at another dispensary and he tells me horror stories about the owners. So I know how good I have it here, boss. Everyone who works at High Society feels the same way."

Stirling hugged her. "You have no idea how much I needed to hear that today."

As usual, when Stirling entered the rec store, she had a burst of pride. High Society lived up to the name—a sleek, upscale modern space, decorated in neutrals with unexpected pops of color. The shelves lined with glass jars of buds were set against a tomato red wall. Tucked in the cannabis consultation area was a deep-cushioned couch in electric blue. She'd balanced class with comfort. The collection of glass paraphernalia arranged by color gleamed like jewels. The display case for the fresh edibles remained glaringly empty, but when the case was stocked, she arranged the ganja goodies like a Parisian *patissere*. Several of their customers referred to High Society as the ultimate adult candy store.

While there was no doubt what was sold in here, there wasn't a single tie-dyed item for sale. No posters of celebrity cannabis smokers adorned the walls. And Bob Marley's music was permanently off the playlist. If cannabis consumption was ever going to be accepted as a societal norm, then keeping alive the counterculture memorabilia and mindset from the 60s and 70s was counterproductive.

So along those lines, Stirling insisted employees—in the store and the grow house—wear uniforms. She hated walking into a dispensary and being unable to discern which people were fellow customers and which ones were store employees. In most places it was hard to differentiate.

She scanned the room, seeing Bob siting on a stool behind the counter. How many customers dismissed him as another employee? Granted, he wore the High Society employee shirt, but the massive man was mean looking. That's why they'd hired him.

Owning a cash-only business had huge drawbacks. Most dispensaries paid cash for everything, including employee wages. After Macon had taken over the dispensary from his client years ago, he'd set up a shell company tied to his law firm to run payroll through so at least their employees could take their paychecks to a bank. The temptation to rob a dispensary of product and cash, especially in the early days, caused owners to hire security guards. Bob was one of six guys in rotation at High Society. On days when she or Kiki had to transport large amounts of cash to pay vendors or tax revenue, they had two men with them at all times.

Stirling waved to Bob and he dipped his chin at her. She noticed the store was at full capacity and they were down an employee on the sales floor. Snagging a black lab coat with the company logo on the pocket, she slipped behind the counter.

Time to earn her cake.

Chapter Ten

"Tell me about *que Sera, Sera.*"

Liam groaned. Stirling was a damn bulldog. Hadn't he told her enough about his past? "You want to talk about that *now?*"

Stirling gestured to where they sat on the floor of the newly remodeled extraction room as they waited for Phil, the company technician, to return from the hardware store. "It's not like we're doing anything else."

"Do you have that condom I gave you?"

"On my person? No. And even if I did, we are not going to fuck on the dirty floor, during the workday when a dozen employees could walk in on us."

"It was merely a suggestion." He whispered, "The floor isn't *that* dirty."

She laughed. "You are ridiculous. But remind me again why you believed this would be a great lunch date?"

Liam crossed his boot over hers. "You don't think staring at a broken valve is fun? There goes my next date night idea where we watch grow lights burn out."

"Liam."

"Sorry I'm punchy. It's just... It's Thursday. We've only seen each other in staff meetings or in passing since Monday." Great. He sounded whiny. Or clingy. Or both.

"That's because my brother is a sadistic fuckhead. Granting us the machine we'd begged for. Warning us that we'd be working closely together. Knowing full well that we're not allowed to exist in the same space at High Society for more than five minutes before one of your people needs you or one of my people needs me. It's a wonder we had time to prank each other at all the past ten months."

"It's very telling that we both prioritized it. I didn't realize how infrequently I actually see you on a daily basis until I wanted to see you."

Stirling rested her head on his shoulder. "That's sweet. Now tell me about your relationship with Miz Duck Lips-Fake Tits."

No more avoiding this discussion.

"You said you worked with her at GreenTech. Was she a fellow lab rat?"

"No. She couldn't cut the master's program at Cal Poly. That should've been my tipoff since I earned my master's in agriculture there in eighteen months."

"Of course you have a master's in agriculture. I should've known a doctorate in microbiology wouldn't be enough. Anyway, Sera worked in...?"

"Client relations. I never understood what that meant except she traveled extensively and her cell phone was surgically attached to her hand."

"Did she recruit you?"

"No. Her father, Sid Greenley, CEO and founder of GreenTech, approached me. At the time I still worked for the company that hired me after I finished my doctorate and I was ready for a career change."

"How long did you work there before you started slipping Sera the test tube?"

"Jesus, Stirling." He laughed. This woman was absolutely unlike anyone he'd ever met. He couldn't remember the last time he'd laughed so much. "I'd been languishing in the lab for a year and a half. Because like you"—he angled his position and kissed the crown of her head—"I killed myself to prove to the suits in charge I was worth the investment. GreenTech was heavily allied with big pharmaceuticals. Insert boring details about secondary research I came across regarding real cannabis and not the artificial compounds we manufactured. I co-opted the information and worked on it during my down time. Anyway, my nosy coworkers were more excited than jealous that I'd isolated a specific anandamide—the natural endocannabinoid that our bodies make—and one of them spilled the seeds to management. That's when Sera took an interest in me."

"And the interest was mutual?"

How much was he supposed to tell her about his former lover?

Stirling briefly lifted her head and said, "No editorializing."

Everything, apparently. "Sera had fake tits and duck lips. How could I not be attracted to her?" he teased.

"Funny. Go on."

"We started fucking. Now I see it for what it was. We were together when she wasn't traveling. She was fascinated by my research—or so I believed, in my arrogance. I wanted to impress her. And I did because her father visited me in the lab and asked to see my research."

"Now I get why you were so resistant to sharing your notes."

Liam bypassed that comment. "Sid made that project my priority. So by the time I'd been employed there two and a half years, I'd successfully cloned plant S219 twenty times, achieving a strain that will manage pain for a variety of ailments."

Stirling got in his face. "I don't need a biological breakdown of your work, Dr. Argent. I want to know how you *felt* about Sera. Did your heart race whenever you saw her? Was she affectionate to you outside of the bedroom? Did you smoke together? Did you buy her flowers and jewelry? Did she take you on business trips? Did you treat her to candlelit dinners? Did you indulge in long, romantic walks on the beach? Did your friends hang out with you as a couple? Did you make plans for a future with her?" Her eyes searched his. "Did you love her?"

"I loved fucking her. But that stopped as soon she'd gotten what she wanted, which was the millions GreenTech got paid for S219. She dropped me so fast it was more comical than pathetic. One weekend I'm fucking her in her bed and she's screaming how much she loves my cock. A week later she's screaming at me to get out of her office and calling me a dick. So no, I didn't love her. But it still stung my pride to know I'd been used and discarded."

Stirling had slumped back against the wall.

He looked at her. "What?"

"Never mind."

Liam turned Stirling's face toward his. "You forced me to tell you this, so you're not allowed to be pissy with me when you don't like what you hear."

"That's the thing. I didn't *hear* anything except that you fucked her and she fucked you over."

He stroked that stubborn jawline. "In retrospect, that's all it was. We never were together in public. She traveled extensively, so I understood that she preferred to spend her weekend at home. I might've bought her Starbucks once. But anything else? Not even dinner. And *que Sera, Sera* literally recoiled when I brought out my stash and she snottily announced that she didn't smoke 'dope.'"

"I kind of hate her."

"Me too. Maybe she and Nick the Prick will cross paths someday. They deserve each other." He swept his thumb across her lower lip. "We deserved better. I think we've found it." He slanted his mouth over hers. At the first touch of his tongue to hers, euphoria similar to a cannabis high rushed through his body. The more times they were together the more right it felt. The more he wanted this feeling.

Liam tried to keep the kiss sweet and reassuring, not let the fact he hadn't kissed her since Monday drive it into I-want-to-fuck-you mode. But the uncertainty of when they'd be alone together again increased their mutual hunger. Need wouldn't be denied. Once the kiss caught fire, no fucking way was he putting it out.

No. Fucking. Way.

Stirling made the sexiest noises when his tongue was buried in her mouth. What noises would she make when his tongue was deep in her pussy, licking her from the inside out?

His cock was on board with that plan.

Even when they paused to take a breath, their lips weren't far apart. And he really loved how quickly she'd adapted to kissing a guy with glasses.

"Liam."

"Uh-huh."

"Will you come with me to the family thing on Saturday night at the ranch?"

Being around all those men who literally wrestled stock for a living... He wondered what kind of reception he'd get. He'd met Stirling's parents before, but not in this state. Where every day he fell deeper in like with their daughter. That thought forced him to cowboy up. "One question. Do I have to wear chaps? Because mine are at the cleaners."

She laughed into his neck.

He really loved that.

"No chaps, boots, hats, or spurs. But I do request you wear those jeans you had on the night you cooked for me."

Puzzled, he eased back to look at her. "Why?"

"Your ass looks fantastic in them, Dr. Booty."

"Can I tell you a secret?" He whispered, "My ass looks even better *out* of them."

Stirling gave him a smacking kiss on the mouth. "Soon." Then she stood and brushed off her pants. "I have a million things to do. You do too. But we can communicate through texts and Snap—"

"The next syllable had better be *ing*...not chat," he warned.

"What do you have against Snapchat?"

"Nothing. As long as I don't have to use it."

She rolled her eyes. "How old are you?"

"Old enough to say *no* to pointless endeavors."

"Fine. I'll text you."

* * * *

By "text" Stirling had meant carrying on entire conversations. Bizarre discussions, which should've been no surprise to him.

Thursday night's texts began with them sending each other funny memes.

Then they shared links to strange scientific discoveries.

That led to snippets of their favorite songs, to discussion of overrated movies, to images of places they'd been and places they'd hoped to go, to food and sports.

The last image she'd sent was a selfie of her in bed, making duck lips.

ME: This is not a come-on, but what are you wearing?

SG: Pajamas, perv.

ME: Seriously, what are those things on your bottoms?

SG: Excuse me?

ME: Your pajama bottoms have cartoons on them?

SG: Not cartoons, animated characters.

ME: Aka—cartoons.

SG: No, the animated character on these is Mulan from the movie *Mulan* and her pet dragon.

ME: Why do you have them?

SG: Because they're comfy.

ME: Stirling. Seriously. That is not a legitimate answer.

SG: Why, Dr. Freud... Are you attempting to psychoanalyze my pajama selection? Like it was a happy time in my childhood and I'm trying to find a connection to that happy child as an adult?

ME: You give me far too much credit. I never think that deep on a personal level. Sorry. Where did you get them?

SG: Why? Do you want a pair?

ME: Hilarious. So an old boyfriend gave them to you?

SG: NO! There is no special significance. I got them on sale at the mall, okay? In fact, I have three other pairs of pajama pants with animated characters on them. Belle, from *Beauty and the Beast*, and *Winnie the Pooh* and Woody from *Toy Story*. Satisfied?

ME: Yes, but those are some crazy pants.

SG: LOL.

ME: That would be a great nickname for you. Crazy pants. It fits on so many levels.

SG: DON'T YOU DARE CALL ME CRAZY PANTS.

ME: I won't. At least not to your face...

SG: LIAM

ME: Kidding. I can't wait to peel those crazy pants off you, hot stuff. Is that better?

SG: Much. Kissy faces to you.

ME: Get some sleep.

Liam had toiled a full day on Friday, wondering if he ought to back out of attending Stirling's sister's party since he'd fallen behind. But Stirling would be upset if he bailed on her, so he'd suck it up and go because she acted like she needed him.

His cell phone buzzed with a text message. He pulled it out of his lab coat pocket and removed his silicone glove.

SG: Let's pretend we just met through an online dating service.

ME: Why?

SG: Because I have questions, dumbass. And I didn't think you'd want to spend our rare face-to-face time together filling out an "Are you compatible?" questionnaire.

ME: I'm with Artie in stage-two grow. There might be a lag time between answers.

SG: LIAR. You're in your lab. I should know because I'm closing the store with Jumanji.

ME: Wrong. I *was* in the lab. I've been out back for two hours.

SG: Whatev. This is how it'll work. I'll type in the question. Then we'll both have thirty seconds to answer.

ME: Got it.

SG: Q1 – Growing up did you have a pet? If yes, what?

ME: No

SG: That wasn't 30 seconds Dr. Cheater!

ME: Fastest answer always wins.

SG: Not in this case. Competitive much?

Liam chuckled. "You have no idea."

Artie stopped checking the flow numbers on the drip system. "Sorry?"

"Nothing. I was just…" Like a dumbass he pointed to his phone.

"Sexting with Stirling?" Artie supplied with a grin.

Don't fucking blush. "What makes you think that?"

"You're walking around smiling despite the fact we're working sixteen-hour days and stage-one grow ended up a total loss."

"And?"

"And no pranks this week from either of you."

"Maybe because we've both been busy working sixteen-hour days?"

"Or maybe because you've been too busy *kissing* boss lady in the break room," Artie said and puckered his lips, smacking out kissing noises.

Never mind the fact Liam blushed as red as the Scarlet Fever buds, what the fuck was wrong with Artie? A grown man—a grandfather, for Chrissake—making kissing noises?

"Don't deny it. Lexa saw you two earlier today. She's a gossip hound."

"Everyone knows?"

He shrugged. "Everyone who worked today. For what it's worth… I think it's great you two are bouncing the bedsprings. Love is what makes life worth living, man."

"Yesterday you said *weed* makes life worth living," Liam pointed out.

Artie just grinned. "Keep sexting with your lady. I got this."

Jesus.

ME: The jig is up
SG: ...the news is out...

Liam laughed again. For fuck's sake. He'd fallen right into that one.

ME: ...they finally found us. Yes, I'm talking about our employees discovering that—
SG: You and I aren't currently fucking? Not news, L. In fact, it's OLD news.
ME: I'm serious. Lexa saw us in the break room today. See if she put a note up on the employee bulletin board because according to Artie, everybody knows.

He watched that "..." for what seemed like forever.

SG: Motherfuck! Jumanji knows about us. He just asked if I wanted to take home a bottle of Foria sensual cannabis oil. Fair warning: I will smoke cannabis and ingest it, but I WILL NOT RUB IT ON MY VAGINA. My vagina doesn't need to relax. My vagina needs to be on edge, tight with anticipation, quivering...

Liam groaned and clicked off his screen. A man could only stand so much.

Artie said, "That good, huh?"

Do not explain to Artie that Stirling is not *sending you pictures of her quivering vagina.*

"Look, Artie—"

Liam's phone buzzed in his hand.

"Better get that," Artie said with a wink.

SG: Are you ignoring me?

ME: Yes. No more conversations about quivering body parts. I mean it.

SG: Great! We can finish our compatibility quiz.

ME: Why? What's the point?

When the "…" stayed on his screen for far longer than a normal message took to type, he braced himself.

SG: What's the POINT? The point is we need to get to know each other. Because we are not IN A REAL RELATIONSHIP until you know a few things about me and I know more about you. Personal things. Stupid things. Funny things. Sexy things. NORMAL things that a man and a woman who have worked together for TEN MONTHS should know about each other, and we don't.

ME: Is this about us going to see your family tomorrow?

Shit. More of the "…" and somehow he knew he'd screwed up.

SG: Liam…honey…baby…sweetie… Do you *want* to have sex with me?

He was so fucked. He'd better make this answer world class. He'd even use a fucking emoji if he had to.

ME: More than I want to take my next breath.

Please answer fast he said to the "…" on the screen.

SG: THEN YOU WILL TAKE THIS MOTHERFUCKING

QUIZ TO THE BITTER FUCKING END AND YOU WILL TELL ME SHIT ABOUT YOURSELF AND YOU WILL ACT GODDAMNED HAPPY TO LEARN SHIT ABOUT ME. YOU DO *NOT* GET TO BITCH ABOUT IT ONE SINGLE BIT BECAUSE I DID THE FIVE THINGS FOR YOU TEST. DO YOU UNDERSTAND? OR ARE YOU PERPETUALLY GOING TO BE DR. NEVER-GONNA-GET-LAID?

"Fine, crazy pants. You didn't have to yell," he muttered.

"Bet you don't call her that to her face," Artie said.

"You're right, because I like my balls where they are."

ME: Where were we in the quiz? I answered that I didn't have a pet. What was your answer?

SG: I grew up on a ranch so I had dogs, cats, horses. Once I even had a pet pig.

ME: Please tell me you named it MACON BACON

SG: LOL

As reluctant as Liam was to admit it, at the end of the two-hour quiz, Stirling had been right. They'd needed to learn the basic dating stuff about each other—not when they were high or working together.

ME: See you tomorrow afternoon. Feel free to bring your crazy pants to sleep in.

SG: Maybe I won't sleep in anything at all.

ME: Even better. Then neither of us will get any sleep.

Chapter Eleven

"What's the story we're telling your family?" Liam asked her.

Stirling floored it to get onto the freeway, holding her response until she'd merged into the traffic leaving Denver. "I haven't thought that far ahead."

"That's not like you."

"We've been a wee bit busy this week at High Society. Besides, I knew we'd have time to kill on the way to the GFR&R."

"Is that Western lingo I should be familiar with?"

"Shorthand for Gradsky Family Ranch and Rodeo." Reaching over, she squeezed his thigh. "Relax. I have enough nervous energy for both of us."

Liam threaded his fingers through hers.

His quiet support humbled her, reinforcing her gratitude that he'd agreed to accompany her this weekend.

"What's the most troubling aspect of this family party for you?"

"Other than the fact that neither my mom nor dad clued me in about this party? But Macon knew? London is my only sister. I should've been involved in some aspect of planning a party for her."

"You get along with your parents?"

"I thought I did."

He aimed his gaze out the window and didn't answer.

"Hey." Stirling snapped her fingers. "Eyes back over here. You don't get to pretend you're suddenly interested in the scenery."

"I'm attempting to get a grasp on the Gradsky family dynamic before I'm thrust into it."

"You make it sound like there'll be bare-knuckle brawling. I assure you that won't happen."

A feigned expression of alarm crossed his face. "I agreed to come on the condition of witnessing family fisticuffs. If that's not a possibility, please turn around and take me back to Denver."

She laughed. "Who even uses the word 'fisticuffs' anymore?"

"I did." Liam kissed her hand. "To bring a smile to your face."

His sweetness was still a shock to her. "Thank you."

"Stirling, what's going on?"

"Blunt truth? It bothers me that my parents haven't come to see me in Denver since they moved closer to me. The rodeo school—"

"GFR&R," he interjected.

"You're catching on, boy. We'll getcha talkin' cowboy in no time."

"Pass. Back to the blunt truth, darlin'."

"I know firsthand how hard it is to run a business and how crucial that first year is. But I came home twice during the holidays. Phone calls, texts, all that...so sporadic it doesn't count. I take some comfort in the fact they've been out of touch with Macon as much as me." A scowl twisted her mouth. "But I can guarantee they haven't been out of touch with London or their grandson Brennen."

Childish much?

"Sorry. That wasn't fair. London works at the ranch. Part of me fears that my parents make up excuses not to see me because whatever pride they had in me vanished when I lost my corporate job and jumped into the cannabis business," she said in a rush. She'd never admitted that to anyone.

"Let's assume for a moment there's some truth to that. Would your parents have lost pride in Macon, too?"

Stirling shook her head. "Macon is an attorney. The cannabis business is a side gig for him. If it fails, all he's out is money. He'll just don one of his hideous three-piece suits and go to his office. I, however..."

"Are a brilliant woman with a master's degree, and racked up years of experience as an agriculture conglomerate executive." Liam brought their joined hands to his lips to kiss her knuckles. "If it comes down to that, Stirling, I have every confidence you'll land on your feet."

She blushed, almost blurting out she hadn't been fishing for compliments.

"I can't imagine your parents aren't proud of your *ganjapreneurial* endeavors." He grinned when she laughed at his terminology. "Especially since they're farmers themselves."

"They grow hay, alfalfa, and corn. Normal farmer crops."

Stirling felt him studying her and said "What?" without taking her eyes off the road.

"Is that why you're insistent on starting an organic farm? Because it's considered more normal—in their eyes—than growing cannabis?"

Liam's perceptiveness startled her.

"Partially. Running an organic farm appealed to me because I could make it my own niche by focusing on supplying to farm-to-table restaurants. I had a romanticized vision of harvesting the exact same variety of beans, tomatoes, squash, and potatoes that my great-great grandparents did. I wanted to feel connected."

"And since your acreage is close to your parents', you'd be part of the same community; hence, they'd see you as an extension of themselves and show parental pride."

"It's not their pride I wanted as much as that family connection. The truth..." God. Did she even want to tell him this? Would he look at her differently?

Liam kissed her hand again. "No judgment, remember?"

"The truth is I've been a shitty, self-centered daughter, singularly focused on me and my goals since I left for college. I rarely came home. Same story when I started grad school. Too busy making my own way. Then when I landed the job at GenAgra, as a big-time executive I had responsibilities they couldn't comprehend. Again, I hardly ever came home. My mom and dad both stopped calling me, because every time they called, I told them it wasn't a good time and I'd have to call them back."

"Did you call them back?"

"A week or two later, when I remembered." Guilt weighed on her whenever she recalled that time in her life. "So weeks stretched into months between phone calls. I had no idea the level of expansion Grade A Farms underwent. When I found out..." Her face heated and she choked back a bitter laugh. "I had the audacity to demand why no one had told *me*."

"Stirling."

She shook her head. *Don't be sweet and supportive right now because I don't deserve it.* "I'd like to brag that I had an epiphany and changed my self-serving ways, but it didn't happen. My job became unbearable. Then when the Nick fiasco occurred, what was the first thing I did? Ran home to my mother. And because she's such an amazing person, she let me cry on her shoulder and complain about my life. The last time I had done that I was a bratty sixteen-year-old. She gave me one piece of advice: *find who you were meant to be.* I ran with it and I haven't looked back."

"Except for now."

"Yes. It sucks to admit this, but I've been out of touch with my parents the last year. Old habits die hard, right? Anyway, I shouldn't be whining because they're throwing a party for London. I love my sister and I'd always hoped as we got older that we could find that bond we had when we were kids." Stirling flashed him a quick smile. "That was the super-long, super-psychoanalytical answer to your question about why I decided organic farming would be the best idea *evah.* I based a monetary investment on a career path that my emotions chose, not my brain."

He lifted his shoulder in a half shrug. "It happens."

"Has it happened to you?"

His non-answer was telling.

"So as if the universe wanted to reiterate that point, after the mess with the infestation, it hit me that as an organic farmer, I'd be dealing with plant diseases, bugs, and Mother Nature on a much larger scale. Two hundred acres of uncertainty. Do I really want that to be my life?" She shot him a sideways glance. "Why can't I just admit I'm happy being fully invested—financially and emotionally—in High Society? Even if the failure of it rests heavier on me than on my brother."

"Then conversely, the success is yours to celebrate too." He chuckled. "I do have an optimistic side. Who knew?"

There are more sides to you than I ever imagined.

"Sorry for veering onto that tangent. I'm sure you don't want to spend this time hearing about my neuroses."

"I could tell you that your neuroses are unfounded…but that's the rub, isn't it?"

She muttered, "I wouldn't believe you."

"Exactly." His fingers squeezed hers. "So *will* you make amends with your parents?"

"Not at a party for my sister." She sighed. "Who am I kidding? I'll probably chicken out and say nothing."

"If it plays out that way, don't beat yourself up."

"Because we agreed lamenting lost opportunities is pointless."

"Only regarding sex," he said in a huskier tone. "Speaking of…"

Her belly swooped. "Yes?"

"Did you bring that condom with you?"

Interesting. So he couldn't see the square outline in the front pocket of her jean skirt. "Maybe. Maybe not."

"I'm to play the 'will we or won't we?' guessing game?"

"No. But you were bragging about having moves that would impress me."

His hard gaze bored into her. "And you want me to prove it."

She smirked. "Only if you want to know where that special condom is." Taunting him was always entertaining. Plus, there wasn't a whole lot of room for seduction as they were speeding down the highway, but it would make the time go faster.

"Challenge accepted."

Sucker.

"Can you keep your eyes on the road when I'm touching you?"

His deep rasping voice fired every sense receptor in her body, blasting her with a punch of sexual heat. "Depends on where you're touching me."

Liam trailed his finger up the inside of her wrist to caress the bend in her elbow. "Just your hand and your arm."

"That's it?"

"Yes."

"Sounds fair."

He traced the bones in the back of her hand with his thumb. "If you'd given me the condom and the choice of when we'd become lovers? I wouldn't have lasted a day, to say nothing of four days."

She hadn't been holding off because of pride or fear, but from lack of opportunity.

Bringing her hand to his mouth again, Liam brushed playful kisses across her knuckles.

Tingles inched up her arm.

"That's why I left the decision to you." His lips glided across her fingers in a lazy zigzag.

"Do you regret that?"

"No." Turning her hand so her palm faced him, he began nibbling below her pinkie, his thumb sweeping a sensual arc on the inside of her forearm. "Nothing compares to the unfettered imagination. You've wondered if my touch will be reverent or rough. Will the connection of our bodies be slow and sensual? Is my lovemaking like molasses, heavy and sweet in the darkness?"

That's where Stirling's thoughts flew. To Liam's body poised above hers, his hard abdomen sliding across the softness of her belly as he slowly thrust in and out of her.

"Or will we join together in a clothes-ripping, hair-pulling frenzy?" Still clasping her hand, he scraped her fingers through the bristly five-o'clock shadow along his jawline. "Desperate to reach that pinnacle of release as our damp bodies slap together in perfect rhythm?"

Stirling started to worry *maybe* she'd been a little cocky about Liam's ability to seduce her as they cruised down the road.

"But this isn't about you," he said. "This is about me. Imagine that *I* get to choose when we fuck, where we fuck, and how we fuck."

She shivered at hearing the sexy growl accompanying the way he said *fuck*.

"I'd want you naked, spread-eagled on my bed."

And...she jerked the wheel.

Paranoid, she spared a look at him. Whew. He hadn't noticed.

"Blindfolded, but not bound," he added.

Wait. What? "Why blindfold me?"

"So your focus is solely on my touch." After he placed an openmouthed kiss on her palm, he slid his lips to the base of her hand, spreading her fingers across his chin and jaw, gripping her arm below her wrist to hold it in place. His breathing had deepened, along with his voice. "I'd watch every quiver, every goose bump, every arch of your back as my hands worshiped you."

"Worshiped?" she repeated.

"Every. Beautiful. Inch."

In her mind's eye she watched Liam's rough-skinned palms smoothing over her breasts and hips as she basked in the possessiveness of his caress.

Liam didn't resume his verbal foreplay, but the continual stroking of his thumb on the inside of her arm was a special kind of sensual torture.

"And then?" she asked him.

"Pardon?"

"What would you do next?"

"Hmm. Let me think."

"For fuck's sake, Liam. This is your fantasy. What happens next?"

Liam lightly rubbed the base of her hand back and forth over the scruff on his chin, his full lips teasing her palm with every pass.

More erotic torment.

A breathless moment and then an electric shock zinged straight between Stirling's legs when Liam speared his hot, wet tongue between her index and middle finger.

She gasped and shifted in her seat.

"Focus on the road," he said as a sexy reprimand.

"I *am.*"

"Don't be cross. I'm getting to the good part." He trailed his lips up the inside of her forearm. "This is how softly I'd kiss up the inside of your thigh."

Don't close your eyes.

"This is how slowly I'd go back down, letting my breath fan over each damp spot my kisses created." His lips followed the path of his words, using her arm to demonstrate. "Savoring the journey." Then he was pushing his wicked tongue between her fingers again. "Until the scent of you drove me mindless. Until..."

Her breath stalled as she waited for him to continue.

"I just had to taste you." Liam opened his mouth over the ball of her thumb and sank his teeth into the smooth flesh, flicking his tongue where her clit would be if he'd settled that naughty mouth between her legs.

Stirling jerked the wheel at the sudden throb in her pussy.

He murmured, "Steady," as he scattered kisses across her forearm.

"Steady? How am I supposed to keep it steady? You bit me! You were just supposed to be touching me!" Maybe he'd believe that the bite threw her and not get cocky about his ability to render her wet with just his mouth on her hand.

"I was touching you with my teeth."

"Touching with teeth is called biting!" *Brilliant comeback, Stirling.*

"You don't say," he murmured again. He licked the bend in her elbow delicately, as if he was tonguing her pussy. Then his teeth were sinking into her skin, the suction of his mouth adding more pressure. When she gasped, he backed off and held her arm closer to her face. "That"—he pointed to the ball of her thumb—"was a nibble. But this one"—he swept his thumb across his teeth marks—"is more of a true bite, wouldn't you agree?"

And…she was done.

No more hate flirting.

No more innuendo flirting.

No more under-the-influence-of-cannabis flirting.

No more text flirting.

No more flirting with disaster in the cab of her truck.

Done. Done. And done.

Almost petulantly she extracted her arm from his hold.

"Stirling?"

She held her hand up in front of his face, letting him know she didn't want to talk.

Surprisingly, he didn't push the issue.

When Stirling took the next exit, she felt his quizzical look, but he said nothing.

When she turned down an unmarked gravel road, he said nothing.

When she parked in a pullout facing an empty field, he said nothing.

But when she killed the ignition, undid her seatbelt, pulled the condom out and slapped it on his chest, he said, "Right now?"

"Right fucking now." She climbed over the console and straddled him. "Your imagination puts mine to shame." After she unbuckled his seat belt, she plucked his glasses from his face and set them on the dash. "I'm wet—which is your fault. And you're gonna do something about it." Stirling feathered soft kisses across his lips as she stared into his eyes. Eyes that had heated to molten silver.

"Unbutton your shirt."

Heart thundering, she leaned back and popped all the snaps open on her Western shirt with one hard tug.

Liam slipped the shirt off and slid his hands around to unhook her bra. His chin was nearly buried in her cleavage as he stripped the bra away. As soon as he glimpsed her hard nipples, a groan of appreciation escaped and he sucked the tip of one between his lips.

Arching into him, Stirling jammed her hands into his hair, holding him in place.

He sucked and bit her nipples. Licked her breasts to please himself, taking what he wanted, what he'd been waiting for.

That made her hotter than she'd ever imagined.

His hands spanned her waist and glided up, his thumbs caressing the bottom swell of her breasts while his mouth alternated between hard and soft sucks, between one nipple and the other.

Stirling felt too confined in her clothes. In her skin. She needed to burn off this lust-fueled energy. Impatient to touch him, she attacked the buttons on his shirt.

He slumped back in the seat, his mouth wet from sucking on her, watching as she undressed him, not uttering a word. The silence between them ratcheted the intensity to another level.

Each button slipping free released more of the musky scent of his skin. She ruffled the springy hair on his chest and felt his belly quiver when she dragged her fingertips along the waistband of his pants.

Liam brought her mouth to his. While the deliciously brutal kiss destroyed the few clear paths of thought she had left, he gripped her ass and lifted her, giving her access to his belt.

Stirling's belt-unbuckling dexterity faltered when Liam's hands cruised up the backs of her bare thighs and beneath her skirt.

He didn't ask permission to touch her. His husky rumble vibrated into the kiss when his fingers stroked her wet panties. He wrenched the material aside and followed her slit from bottom to top.

Gently separating her folds, he positioned the tip of his thumb on her clit, drawing a tight circle, over and over. Letting his nail randomly flick that swollen nub, he added a quick bite of pain to the pleasure he was pushing her toward.

Stirling's legs were shaking. She abandoned her quest to depant Liam, too absorbed in the erotic havoc surging through her.

When he slid two fingers into her pussy, she wrenched her head back, breaking the kiss. She started to ride his hand, trying to force those fingers deeper, impatient to reach that tipping point into bliss.

But Liam stayed her movement, his hand tightly squeezing her hip, a silent warning he was giving her pleasure rather than her taking it.

Stirling let go and entrusted him to drive her closer to the edge.

His breath fanned across her collarbone as he scattered kisses up her neck.

Of course he'd discovered the surefire way to send her soaring to orgasm—firm-lipped bites at the intersection of her shoulder and neck.

As soon as he set his mouth on her, she came undone at the seams. A swift unraveling as her interior muscles spasmed around his thrusting fingers and her clit pulsed beneath the steady pressure of his thumb. She shuddered and shook, tingles zipping down her spine, spinning her around and around in that vortex of pleasure until it spit her back out, leaving her hazy headed, her entire being throbbing as she gasped for breath.

The window had fogged over. The glass was cool and wet beneath her hand where she'd braced herself.

The humid air in the cab heated the fervor between them; it was hard to breathe and there was no need to speak. Liam merely pressed the condom into her palm and raised his hips.

Still shaking, Stirling managed to yank his pants and briefs to his knees. She tore open the wrapper and reached between them to roll the condom down his cock.

Liam's eyes were wild. He curled his hand around the back of her neck, bringing her close enough to scrape his teeth up her throat. He gritted out, "Turn around," into her ear, causing a fresh batch of goose flesh to cover her skin.

Her heart kicked up a beat or twenty when she was facing forward with her hands braced on the dash and her knees beside Liam's thighs.

Then Liam moved the seat back.

Way back.

Thank God for club cabs and bucket seats.

Instead of reclining in the seat, Liam scooted forward to the very edge…and pulled her back, impaling her with one deep stroke.

She automatically arched up and groaned. Oh yeah. That's what she needed.

He groaned too, one hand circling her hip, the other grabbing a handful of dreads to hold her in that position as he drove his shaft in a little further with every thrust.

Sex had never, ever, ever been this good. Especially not the first time.

Stirling wouldn't have blamed him if he hammered into her until he climaxed. But of course he didn't. He stopped, fully bottomed out inside her and reached for her hand, bringing her fingers to his mouth to suck on them.

Which…that sexy move alone caused a throb deep in her pussy.

Then he upped the eroticism ante, pulling her hand between her legs to where his cock was lodged inside her and dragged her fingers to her clit.

Touch yourself since I can't. Come again. Come when I'm inside you.

The words weren't spoken aloud, but she heard them nonetheless. As soon as Stirling began a little self-love, Liam clutched her hip and her dreads and took her to pound town.

It was fucking glorious.

She might've passed out for a few seconds when her second orgasm rolled over her like a rogue wave that left her clinging to the dash in the aftermath.

Liam slammed into her faster until his entire body went rigid...and he came with an actual roar.

A roar.

Stirling could totally fucking love this guy.

He slumped forward, his forehead nestled in the small of her back, his rapid breaths drying the sweat that had pooled there.

Once she sensed Liam's brain was back online, she dismounted and shifted to face him. "So we have that going for us."

He laughed and gently pulled her to his mouth—via her hair—for a swoon-worthy kiss that curled her toes in her boots.

"Good thing we didn't fuck by the extraction machine because the sexual heat between us would've blown that sucker sky high."

"Agreed. Look, I need to move, this is killing my back." That's when she noticed his smirk. "What?"

"We had sex in a truck. I'm practically a real cowboy now."

After smooching his lips, she climbed over the center console. "I'm a real cowgirl now, too, because that was my virgin ride in any vehicle."

That surprised him. "Another first we have in common."

She'd tracked down most of her clothes. "Hey, is my underwear over there?"

Liam sighed. "Yes, but don't get mad." He dangled the white bikinis between them.

One leg opening was stretched out beyond repair. "Guess I'm going commando."

Stirling resituated herself and started the truck.

"How much farther?" he asked.

"We'll be there before you know it."

Chapter Twelve

Liam let the silence last five minutes before he said, "Stirling, stop acting weird."

She spared him a haughty look. "I'm not acting weird. I'm concentrating on driving."

Liam let it go, refusing to be one of those "Was it good for you, baby?" kind of lovers. Stirling came twice. That made it pretty goddamn spectacular for both of them.

He closed his eyes and immediately his brain replayed images of them. Her skin turning rosy from the heat they generated. The taste of her skin. The scent of sex. Her nails digging into the dashboard. The sexy sound she couldn't hold in when he rolled his hips and hit the right spot.

"You're thinking about it, aren't you?"

He looked at her. "Of course I am. Aren't you?"

"Yes." Her hands tightened on the steering wheel. "I want to turn around and spend the next two days naked in your bed."

"It is an exceptionally comfortable bed. Sturdy too."

"You'd be okay if I whipped a U-ie and headed back to Denver?"

"Yes. But the question is whether *you'd* be happy with that decision."

She scowled at him. "I hate when you're the voice of reason."

Liam laughed.

After another few minutes of silence and no physical change in direction, Liam said, "Do you know anything about this party?"

"Nothing. We've been so swamped this week I forgot that Macon's admin was supposed to email me his playlist and instructions. I logged into all my email accounts and evidently he neglected to send it. Now I have that worry on top of everything else."

"What kind of music does your sister listen to?"

"Country."

"Find a Pandora station and plug your phone into the sound system. Instant party music. If people stop dancing or start complaining about the music, just change the station."

"I love it when you're the voice of reason," she said dryly.

"It's a blessing and a curse."

A few moments later she said, "Thank you for coming with me. I know it's my family and I shouldn't be all weird about going to it, but I am. Having you there... I need that. Even more than I want to admit."

Liam reached for her hand. He didn't say anything. He didn't need to.

"I did get a text from my mom yesterday, making sure I planned to come. But she didn't mention if the occasion called for formal dress or whether gifts were expected."

"I can't remember the last time I wore a tux."

"I'd love to see you in a black one. I bet you look dashing and debonair."

"Flattery, Miss Gradsky"—he kissed her hand—"will definitely get you laid tonight."

An enormous sign for the Gradsky Rodeo School loomed ahead. A sign that Stirling cruised right past without slowing or tapping the brakes.

"Change your mind?"

"No. That's the public entrance. We'll take the back road and stop at my parents' house first."

A frown wrinkled his brow. "Was I at your parents' place during the open house? So much was going on that night, everything was a blur."

She shook her head. "Their home wasn't part of the tour. They keep it private." She turned right and stopped for the gate to open.

The blacktop meandered through the woods. Once they cleared the forest, a meadow opened up where the Gradskys had built their home. While the house was large—two stories with a covered porch that ran the length of it—the structure was smaller than he'd expected, given the immense size of the buildings in their rodeo complex.

"Home sweet home," Stirling said after she'd parked.

"It looks like a nice place." Liam groaned. "Talk about stating the obvious."

She smiled. "It *is* a nice place. They love it here. It's their home now."

"But?"

"But it's not my home. I grew up on the southern ranch. When I return to visit, it isn't the same because *they're* not there, so it doesn't feel like home either."

"The apartment complex that Gramma and I lived in is gone. Bulldozed for a shopping center."

"Does that bother you?"

"No. Like you said, she's not there and she's what made it home for me."

The look Stirling gave him… For the first time he understood what *heart-melting* meant.

"Anyway, let's grab our bags and see what room Mom stashed us in."

"Don't we wait out here for the hired hands to grab our luggage?" Liam asked.

When Stirling realized he was joking, she smiled. "I love that you do that for me."

"Do what?"

"Create a funny or annoying distraction. It takes the sting out when I realize that my parents aren't bounding down the steps to welcome me."

Liam cupped her chin in his hand. "I'm irritated by their poor choice not to greet their beautiful daughter with open arms." His lips lingered near hers. "Let's show them our displeasure by getting high in your room and partaking in loud, wild sex."

"Partaking?" Stirling grinned. "What quaint Victorian phrasing, Dr. Argent."

Watching her eyes, he pressed his teeth into her bottom lip and flicked his tongue over the mark. "Does fucking you raw and dirty sound better?"

"God yes."

He kissed her. "Let's go."

She opened the tailgate and Liam unloaded the three bags. They'd stepped onto the porch when a young woman bounded toward them.

"Hi. Stirling? I've been waiting for you. I'm Calliope Morgan."

"Hello, Calliope. Sorry we're early."

Liam discreetly studied this stranger sent to meet Stirling. A pretty little thing, in that fresh-faced country girl way, wearing jeans, a rhinestone shirt, and boots. Her brown hair hung in a braid long enough to brush her waist. Hard to nail down her exact age... She could be anywhere from sixteen to her mid-twenties.

"Where is everyone?" Stirling asked.

"They're at the recreation center." Calliope shoved her hands in her back pockets. "Berlin had last-minute stuff to do, so she asked me to get you settled." Her gaze moved to Liam. "Umm...but she didn't mention you'd be bringing a guest."

He offered his hand. "Pleased to meet you, Calliope. I'm Dr. Liam Argent, Stirling's lord and master."

Shock crossed Calliope's face. The blush reddening her cheeks only emphasized her freckles.

Stirling shoved him aside. "Behave, Dr. Asshat." She smiled at Calliope. "My partner takes his jokes too far. We'll be staying in the same room."

Partner? That's what she was calling him now?

"Okay. Berlin has you in the green room at the end of the hallway." Calliope checked her watch. "There's an hour before things get underway."

"My mother didn't leave word about me coming to help her set up?"

"No. I have strict instructions to tell you to relax and freshen up. One of the ranch hands will pick us up in a golf cart and we'll ride over together."

While this situation seemed odd, it was pointless for Stirling to argue, but that appeared to be her plan. Liam ran his hand up her back. "We could both stand to freshen up. Thank you, Calliope." He pressed a kiss to Stirling's temple. "Lead the way."

"I'll be in the kitchen if you need anything." Calliope ducked around the corner.

Liam flicked a cursory glance at the interior of the house. He'd much rather watch Stirling's ass as she angrily sashayed up the curved staircase.

At the top of the stairs, she booked it down a long hallway and disappeared through a doorway.

He took his time getting to their room, checking out the artwork that adorned the walls and the Western sculptures displayed on hand-carved columns. A full five minutes had passed before he rolled the suitcases into the room and closed the door.

Stirling stopped pacing long enough to demand, "Did you get lost?"

"We have an hour to kill. I looked around."

"We *don't* have an hour. I don't give a damn what Calliope says. We're going to the recreation center now."

"No, we aren't."

"Fine. Stay here. But I'm going."

"We're both staying here." His fingers circled her wrists. He towed her along until the backs of his legs hit the mattress. "We're alone in a room with a bed and have an hour to kill. Whatever shall we do?"

"But—"

Perching on the edge of the bed, he said, "You love it when I create a distraction for you. So strip."

"Liam."

"Do it. I want to see every inch of you before I put my mouth to good use. If you want me to kiss you, lose the clothes so I can ditch my glasses."

"This sounds like a distraction for *you*." Her dreads swung behind her back after she tossed her shirt aside. Doing a reach around, she unhooked her bra and whipped it to the floor. Her beautiful tits swayed as she braced a hand against the wall and removed her right cowgirl boot. Then her left. With a coy grin she flipped her skirt up, giving him a peek at her pussy. Then she spun around, bent over, and treated him to a peek of her ass.

Before Stirling was upright, Liam was behind her, unzipping her skirt, pushing it to her feet. "So fucking hot, Stirling."

"Kiss me."

He placed his glasses on the closest horizontal surface. Then both of his hands roamed over her, greedy to explore all of this sweet flesh, following the curves of her breasts, her belly, and her hips as he dragged his mouth from below her ear to the edge of her shoulder.

She trembled when he scraped his teeth along that same path.

The scent of her hair, her skin, her arousal was ultimate high.

Turning her to face him, he captured her mouth in a sensual kiss. Soft tongue and softer lips. A gentle nip of his teeth. A teasing lick. Keeping his touch gentle as his fingertips lightly drew circles on her breasts. His thumb stroked her belly and he rubbed his jean-clad thigh against the outside of her bare leg.

He quelled the urge to beat on his chest like an animal when her body yielded to his every touch. Her sounds of pleasure weakened his resolve to take this slow.

Liam broke the kiss and rested his forehead to hers, trying to mask the fact he was breathing hard.

Don't hide this. Let her see how strongly she affects you.

"What's wrong?" Her fingertips traced the line of his jaw. "You're kind of shaky."

"Nothing is wrong. But if I don't get my mouth on your pussy in the next minute, there's a good chance I'll die."

Stirling released a sultry laugh. Then she peppered kisses across his jawline, stopping at his ear to whisper, "Well then, let me save your life." She pushed down on his shoulders until he dropped to his knees.

A gentleman would've said something sexy and complimentary before taking that first taste.

Not Liam.

A primal instinct overtook him completely.

He shoved her thighs apart and buried his face into her creamy folds, his mouth open wide, his upper teeth pressed into her mound, his tongue pushing into her pussy deep, lapping up every bit of ambrosia and diving back in for more.

Again and again and again.

Stirling fisted her hands into his hair and held on.

When she released a sharp cry, he froze.

That hadn't sounded like a cry of bliss.

Because you are eating her like this is your last meal.

Christ. He was fucking *growling*. He needed to calm the fuck down.

He retreated to temper his raging hunger for her with soft nibbles and delicate licks as he nuzzled her swollen tissues. Sucking her clit and dropping kisses on the downy blond strip of hair covering her mound.

Four sharps tugs on his hair got his attention. Alarmed, he looked up at her.

"Don't."

"Don't what?"

"Overthink this. If you were too rough, I'd tell you. Give me back the guy who might die if he doesn't get his mouth on my pussy."

"You liked that." A statement. Not a question.

"I loved it." Stirling lowered to her knees. She held his face in her hands and ravaged his mouth. Licking the taste of herself from his lips, sucking it from his tongue. Rubbing her body against his. She released his lips long enough to say, "I taste good on you."

"Let me—"

Another tongue-tangling kiss ended that half-assed protest.

And Stirling proceeded to drive him out of his fucking mind. When she rubbed his nipples, it felt like she'd opened an erotic conduit to his ass and his balls. His skin seemed to shrink with each teasing sweep of her thumb. When she used her tongue... Christ, it felt like she was licking his entire body.

Enough.

He stood, plucked her off the floor and set her on the bed.

She cocked her head when he yanked his T-shirt off. "Change in plans?"

"I'll come back to the pussy eating later." He shed his jeans and briefs, and then bent to retrieve a condom from his luggage.

Stirling whistled. "Look at you, Dr. Hottie. All cut muscles and an awesome dick."

Liam slipped the condom on and joined her on the bed, stalking her as she scrambled up toward the headboard. He paused between her legs. Keeping his gaze on hers, he swirled his tongue around her clit and down to where all that sweetness pooled. "You're wet enough to take me."

No argument from her.

On his way up the bed, he stopped to lash his tongue across her nipples.

She squirmed beneath him. But she didn't beg for more. Or less.

He planted his hands beside her head and skimmed his body over hers.

A breathy sigh escaped as she twined herself around him, arms, legs, hair. All she had to do was cant her hips...

And he surged inside.

"God. That is so good."

Her hands explored his arms and chest and shoulders as he moved in her and above her. Rolling her pelvis to meet his every deep stroke.

The smooth arch of her neck was impossible to resist. A groan rumbled free when the taste of her skin—lemons and sunshine—hit his tongue.

His steady pace wasn't enough so he picked up the speed.

The bed started to squeak. Before he could return to a slower rhythm, Stirling slapped his ass and murmured, "Gimme that dirty, loud sex you promised."

Seeing the passion and joy on her beautiful face, all for him... Liam's overwhelming urge to prove himself worthy resulted in him breaking out his best porn move, swiveling his hips on the upstroke, grinding against her on the downstroke.

"Yes," she gasped. "That. Don't ever stop doing that." She urged him on with the scratch of her nails down his back.

Their mouths would meet and part. Sharing a tender kiss. A kiss that bordered on brutal. Ebb and flow. Perfection. He'd found it, even when he never really believed it existed. But it did. Here in this space and time with her.

The way Stirling held her body changed. Her stomach tightened, the bow in her lower back deepened. Her knees squeezed him harder.

He put his mouth to her ear and growled, "Give it to me."

"Liam."

"All of it, Stirling." He added an extra grind at the end of every bed-rattling thrust.

Sweat dripped into his eyes but he didn't tear his gaze away from her face as she started to come.

Her low moan got louder. She set her teeth on his shoulder to muffle it.

He shuddered from the sharp prickles of pleasure racing across his skin after her bite. The pressure of her pussy muscles contracting around his dick... He was done for.

He didn't just blow; he erupted like a volcano.

The world spun. Hazy gray space obscured his vision. His arms shook but he couldn't stop the short jabs of his cock into that tight haven.

His mouth was bone dry. His skin was damp. He had a cramp in the back of his calf. His abs ached. Fuck, even his hair hurt.

Still...Liam felt nothing short of invincible.

Stirling bumped her pelvis up.

He opened his eyes.

"There you are," she said softly. "Where'd you go?"

"Sex as Nirvana isn't a myth."

"Aha. I thought we reached transcendence. And without chemical stimulants."

Liam nestled his face into her neck and breathed her in.

She swept her hands down his back. "Let's stay here. If they ask what happened to us, we'll tell them we were exhausted from traversing the astral plane."

He lifted his head. "If we tell them that, they'll assume we got too baked to leave the room."

"There's a plan."

"Stirling."

"Gotta face the music. Literally."

"'Fraid so." He pressed a kiss on her forehead and then on her mouth. "Will I lose my status as Dr. Aloof if I say I'm crazy about you?"

Her eyes softened. "Yes. But that's a good thing because the feeling is mutual."

Liam eased off her and casually walked to the garbage can to ditch the condom. But inside he was jumping around, pumping his fist in victory. If he kept grinning like an idiot his face would hurt from smiling too.

Be cool.

He ran his hand through his hair, wondering if he could skip a shower. "Will it take you long to get ready?"

"I have half a mind to wear my Pooh pajama bottoms to this shindig."

"Not your finest clothing option, crazy pants."

Stirling draped her forearm across her eyes. "That name fits today. Pretty soon the sex buzz will wear off and I'll be back to hand wringing and pacing."

"You need another distraction." Liam pulled out a plastic baggie from his shaving kit and crawled back on the bed. "Luckily, I can help with that. Open wide."

"You'd better not shove your dick in my mouth right now," she warned.

"Would you bite?"

"Yes."

"Might be worth it to see these pretty pink lips wrapped around my cock."

"Liam!"

He laughed. "I'm serious. This is not a prank. Open your mouth."

She shifted her arm to watch him suspiciously, but she opened her mouth.

Liam dropped a gummy bear in and blocked her from spitting it out.

Then he popped a gummy in his own mouth. "See? I won't make you do something I'm not willing to do myself."

"This doesn't bode well for our relationship since this is the second time you've slipped me a mickey, pal."

"Mickey. Who even uses that word anymore?"

"Minnie Mouse does," she said with a snicker.

"Hysterical. I heard these gummies work fast but not that fast."

"Whatever. Get dressed. Our hour is almost up."

He bent down and picked up the T-shirt he'd been wearing today.

A naked Stirling hopped off the bed and his train of thought vanished. He could not believe he was here with this beautiful, brilliant goddess.

She said, "Not that one."

"What's wrong with it?" He loved the saying on his T-shirt: *The Good Thing About Science Is That It's True...Whether Or Not You Believe In It.*

"Nothing. But I'm a dreadlock-adorned bohemian who owns a marijuana dispensary. You're my arm candy, baby, so you need to look the part of my hot rebel man. Wear something that shows off those sexy tattoos."

He groaned after he opened his suitcase. "I was in such a hurry I forgot to pack my dress clothes."

"Show me what you brought."

Grumbling, he unsnapped the straps that were supposed to be holding his dress clothes. The other shirt he'd packed was part of his workout gear, a sleeveless nylon-cotton style, resistant to wrinkles. When he faced Stirling, she was gaping at him. "What now?"

"That's how you pack for an overnight?"

"That's how I pack for everything. Isn't that standard?"

She laughed and unzipped her suitcase.

Somehow he masked his horrified expression. Crazy pants had just wadded up clothing and shoved it in without order. Nothing was folded. She'd even mixed shoes in with the clothes. Should he force himself to say something...nice?

Stirling's arms came around him. "Since you haven't been to my place, I can assure you that I don't live in a pigsty. I'm kind of a neat freak. But after years of traveling and having to iron suits because they always ended up wrinkled, I let go of order."

"You have to fit your rebelliousness in where you can, Miss Gradsky." A vivid orange article of clothing hung out and he tugged it free from the rest of the clothes in her suitcase. A pair of her crazy pajama pants. But these… He read the writing beneath the cartoonish character out loud. *"Boys are stupid throw rocks at them."* His eyes met hers. "Seriously, Stirling? You paid for these?"

"No." She snatched them away. "Nana gave them to me after I dumped Nick the Prick, okay?"

"But you were planning on wearing them tonight?"

"Maybe."

He snatched them back. "Maybe not."

"Liam."

"You're not wearing these tonight. Put them on when you're watching rom-coms with your girlfriends and doing each other's nails. But never with me, all right?"

"What is the big deal?"

"Would you be offended if *my* pajamas said: *Girls are stupid throw rocks at them?*"

"Yes, but that is different. Men stone women to death. Women don't throw rocks."

"But little girls do," he said softly. He dropped the pajamas on the floor and snagged his shaving kit on the way to the bathroom.

Way to admit to your loser past.

He braced his hands against the countertop and took a couple of deep breaths.

When Liam raised his head and looked in the mirror, he didn't see the athletic, confident thirty-five-year-old man he'd become. He saw a skinny ten-year-old runt, his eyes enormous beneath eyeglass lenses as thick as the bottom of a pop bottle. Glasses he'd carefully taped together after Jana Oster had hit him in the face with a rock. His glasses had gone flying and he'd crawled on the ground until he found them. While he'd inspected the lenses, silently praying they weren't broken, Jana had continued to pelt him with rocks and insults. He'd ended up with bruises on his arms, the backs of his calves, and the top of his head. But not on his face, thankfully, because his gramma would have demanded to know what happened.

He'd never told her.

He'd never told anyone.

He kept those memories buried most days. He hated that

something as trivial as a phrase on a pair of pajamas could make him overreact.

But did you?

Two soft knocks sounded and the door slowly opened. Stirling didn't say a word; she just ducked under his arm and wrapped herself around him.

He held on.

She whispered, "I'm sorry," against his chest.

"It's all right."

When Stirling tilted her head back, tears shimmered in her eyes.

His stomach tightened at the humiliating thought that she felt sorry for him.

"It's not all right. You had every right to point out the cruelty and reverse discrimination. I'm throwing those crazy pants away."

Liam wiped away a tear. "You don't have to do that."

"Yes, I do. I can't right the wrongs of your past, Liam, but I'd never keep something that brings back awful memories."

He kissed the top of her head. "Thank you."

"Did you ask me if I bought those pajamas because you feared I might've been like the girl who hurt you? The pajamas were a reminder of how fun it'd been to bully and belittle someone when I was a kid?"

I don't know.

"I wasn't a mean girl, Liam. I was awkward. I'm *still* awkward."

"We have that in common."

Stirling kissed his chest, above his heart. "We have a lot in common."

Not as much as she thought. Liam had no idea how to do this family thing. Granted, he'd had his gramma, but that was it. Someone like Stirling, who'd grown up in an environment with siblings, cousins, aunts, and uncles, wouldn't understand why he'd freaked out at the idea of being thrust into the middle of it.

Truth was he hadn't brought those gummies for her. He'd brought them for himself.

On the drive here he'd silently panicked when she'd confessed her family problems. When she'd reached the point that he'd run out of anything resembling advice to offer her, he'd seduced her instead.

And now he couldn't tell her his issues because he was here to support *her.*

"Liam?"

He looked down into her beautiful face and those eyes filled with concern for him, wondering for the hundredth time how he'd gotten so lucky. He did not want to fuck this up. He smiled. "Sorry. I think the gummy bear is kicking in."

"I hope mine kicks in soon, because we need to get ready."

Chapter Thirteen

Two minutes after Stirling and Liam stepped onto the porch, a four-person ATV pulled up.

A cowboy Stirling hadn't seen before exited the driver's side. He offered his hand first to Liam. "Hey. I'm Justin. I work at the Gradsky Ranch. You must be Stirling."

Calliope stomped down the stairs. "Are you kidding me right now? *That* is Stirling. She is Chuck and Berlin's *daughter*."

Silence.

Justin faced Stirling, his handsome face tomato red. "I am sorry, Miss Gradsky. No offense. I've only worked here a few months. I'm still figuring things out."

"No worries. This is my partner, Liam Argent."

"Pleasure to meet you, sir."

"You as well, Justin."

"We probably better get goin'."

Liam patted his chest where his pocket protector would be. He seemed lost without it.

So adorably dorky. Would she still find that cute in fifty years?

Her brain started to flood her body with panic, tension, and fear. She wasn't sure they'd be together fifty days, to say nothing of fifty years.

Just then the magic gummy bear threw a blanket on those thoughts, smothering them completely.

Liam adjusted his glasses. "I left my cell phone upstairs. Be right back."

Yeah, she blatantly watched his ass as he walked away; it looked damn fine in those jeans. His jeans, coupled with the sleeveless gray T-shirt that put those fascinating tattoos on display? And the sexy way his hair fell over his glasses? Hotness. She really felt like she'd be walking into the party with man candy on her arm.

Her body sated, her mind at rest, Stirling walked a few steps and leaned against the wooden post, breathing in the mountain air and basking in this rare serenity.

Which of course was immediately shattered.

"God. Do you have to be so embarrassing?" Calliope hissed. "You thought *Stirling* was a guy? That is not a guy's name."

"What about Sterling Sharpe, who played for the Packers? Or Sterling Archer?"

Calliope had no response for that except a loud huff.

"Wow. So you *don't* know everything. Next time you spout off, little girl, remind yourself you could learn a thing or two from your elders."

Liam exited the house. "Sorry. I'm ready."

Stirling and Liam sat in the back. They'd just started down the paved path that led to the Gradsky complex when Calliope turned around to address Liam. "So what kind of doctor are you? Because I have this rash—"

"I'm not a medical doctor. I have a doctorate in microbiology."

Calliope's lips formed an O of surprise. "To be honest, I'm not even sure what that means. Sounds like a class I probably would've skipped."

"Or failed," Justin added with a snicker.

"Shut it and drive. I wasn't talking to you."

"I could be so fuckin' lucky," he shot back.

Liam muttered, "Harsh."

"What sort of work do you do for my parents?" Stirling asked Calliope.

"Whatever they want me to do." She grinned.

Stirling couldn't help but grin back. The girl was a doll. A chattering doll, as it turned out.

"This week I've mostly been cleaning. Last week I filled in as a ranch hand with grumpy over there." She gestured with her head to Justin and he took his eyes off the road to scowl at her. "Next week I might be takin' care of the animals."

They hit a bump. Calliope yelped as she went airborne.

Justin grabbed the back of her jacket. She scrambled for a hold on the roll bar as Justin hit the brakes—both of which kept her from bouncing out on her head.

"Would you please park your ass in the seat?" Justin snapped. "You about gave me a goddamned heart attack."

"I'm fine. Keep movin', Daddy-o. We're on Berlin time and if we're late, I'm rolling on you."

Stirling covered a laugh with a cough.

Calliope half turned to study her.

"Do I have something on my face?" *Or maybe a hickey or two on my neck where Dr. Hoover set his mouth on me?*

Not that she'd complain about that.

Ever.

"No. And this will sound weird, but your mom has been telling me about all the awesome things you've done and how you were driven to succeed even when you were a kid." She paused. "That sounds just like my little sister Chelsea. Not the dreads or the kickin' clothes, but she has that same drive."

Her mother had been talking about her to the employees? "Really?"

"Yeah. Chels is a soccer player, not a business whiz like you. She's dying to play pro soccer now, but our mom is like... You are going to college first."

"You shoulda listened to your mom too," Justin said.

Calliope rolled her eyes. "There wasn't money for me to go. Besides, nothin' wrong with bein' a bartender."

"You're tendin' bar tonight too?" Justin demanded.

"Yep. See if you can keep up, old man."

When Stirling saw the peak of the barn, she waited for that panicked feeling to pop up, but the magical gummy bears just tucked in the corners of the blanket more tightly.

Calliope's cell phone buzzed. After she read the message, she elbowed Justin. "Change of plans."

He nodded.

"Take the shortcut."

"What shortcut?"

"That one." Calliope pointed.

"That is *not* a shortcut."

"Yes, it is! Turn now or we'll miss it."

Justin hit the brakes. He patted the steering wheel. "See this? This means I decide which way we're going, shortstuff, not you. And we ain't takin' what you call the shortcut."

"You are so stubborn!"

"Like that's news," Justin scoffed.

They started moving again…at a crawl.

"You are doing this on purpose."

"Safety first, little girl."

"Omigod, I am not a little girl! You make me want to scream!"

Justin didn't acknowledge Calliope's frustration. He just kept putzing along.

Calliope leaned over and screamed almost directly in Justin's ear.

He didn't jump but Stirling and Liam did.

Holy shit. She hadn't been expecting an actual scream.

Stirling and Liam exchanged a look.

Justin and Calliope continued to argue with gusto, ignoring them completely.

Liam put his mouth on her ear. "Were we as annoying as the bicker twins?"

"Afraid so. But I only screamed once, when you put that rubber rat in the box of straws in the break room. And you weren't even there to hear it."

"Wrong. I heard that scream all the way in the lab. You would've deafened me had it been in my ear."

"No one helped me pick up the straws, lest you prank *them*."

"I was only interested in pranking you, beautiful." He twined one of her dreads around his palm. "The octagonal dome you engineered from those straws was perfect, even if you did hang a LEGO man in a lab coat from the center of the structure."

She snickered. "At the time it was cathartic to X-out the eyes and wrap a string around its little bitty neck. But now? I'd put a LEGO woman with dreads next to it." On impulse, she kissed him. Twice. "I'm crazy about you. Have I mentioned that?"

"I don't believe so. Maybe you'd better say it again."

"Crazy, crazy, crazy about you." She punctuated each crazy with a kiss.

"That isn't the gummy bear speaking?"

"Do gummy bears speak? Do they sound like that bear in *Ted?* What was his name?"

"Ah…Ted? I love that movie."

"So how long have you two been together?" Calliope interrupted.

Liam said, "And she's *baaaaack*," under his breath.

Stirling released a tiny snort. "Gosh, what's it been...seven days?"

"Eight fantastic days," Liam corrected with a growl.

Calliope's gaze moved back and forth between them. "Does London know you've got a boyfriend? Because I thought she planned to fix you up with someone."

"Calliope, shut up," Justin snarled. "You don't say shit like that to people. Your mama raised you better than that."

"What? I'm just making conversation."

The recreation center came into view as they rounded the corner.

"Here's where we exit this crazy train," Stirling said to Calliope. "Let us out here. We'll walk."

"No can do. My orders are front door delivery."

When Justin muttered something, Calliope lit into him again.

Stirling had had enough. She released an ear-piercing whistle.

Justin slammed on the brakes. He and Calliope gaped at her.

"Here's a piece of advice. Working with family is the hardest thing you'll do. I work with my brother every day. Sometimes I want to scream at him. But I don't *lit-er-al-ly* scream at him, Calliope. Our disagreements happen behind closed doors. Never in front of employees or customers." She addressed Calliope. "I can see that your dad embarrasses you and it probably sucks working together so closely because he treats you like a child—"

"Whoa, whoa, whoa, there." Calliope made a timeout sign. "Justin is not my *dad.*"

Justin pointed at Calliope. "I told you that's what people would think. I *told* you. That's why—"

"You're a chickenshit, Justin Donohue." Calliope tossed her hair. "And like I told you, I don't care what people think."

He hit the gas.

Liam muttered, "Not enough gummy bears in the world to deal with this."

"No kidding."

Stirling saw her mother pacing outside the doors to the recreation center.

When they *finally* arrived, her mom practically ran toward the ATV. "Stirling! Sweetheart, I'm so thrilled you're here."

"Mom." Stirling hugged her tightly. No matter what happened

tonight, she had to carve out more time for her family.

Her mother released her. "Sweetheart, are you crying?"

"Yeah. I just realized how much I miss you."

"Oh, honey. I miss you too."

"And I want things to change. Weeks shouldn't pass between phone calls, Mom. Months shouldn't pass between visits."

"I'm in complete agreement. Let's—"

"I want you to be proud of me even if I don't become an organic farmer."

Her mom's eyes widened.

Liam murmured, "Take a breath because I already gave you a chill pill."

God, she *was* babbling. Stirling inhaled deeply, relaxing into Liam's touch as he rubbed circles on her back. "Sorry, Mom. It's just..."

Her mom reached for her hand. "We have lots to talk about. And we will. I promise. Just not right now, okay?"

"Okay."

"What a darling dress. The navy blue suits you. And the daisies on it." She smiled. "You've always loved daisies."

"Where's Dad?"

"He's inside." Her mother looked at Liam. Then at Stirling. "Dr. Argent. It's lovely that you could join us."

"I'm happy to be here with Stirling, Mrs. Gradsky. Please call me Liam."

With Stirling. No way could her mom misinterpret that.

"And you must call me Berlin." Then she looped her arm through Stirling's and they walked to the doors, Liam following close behind.

It was weird that no one was out here smoking. In fact...where were all the people? This was supposed to be a party. Plus, it took a village to run the rodeo school so it never looked like a ghost town.

"Liam, would you be a dear and open the door?"

"Of course, Berlin."

Stirling kept her eyes on Liam's bare arm, watching his biceps ripple beneath that kick-ass tat when he jerked hard on the door.

A pitch-black entryway greeted them when they stepped inside. "Did the power go out?"

"Not exactly."

The lights came on and a hundred people were spread out in front of her. They all yelled, "Surprise!"

Stirling actually turned around and checked to see if there was someone behind her.

Everyone laughed.

"Yes, sweetheart, this party is for you."

Then her dad started singing, "Happy Birthday" and everyone joined in.

Trying to hide her shock, she leaned into Liam and he held her up. After the group finished the last birthday verse and everyone was clapping and whistling, Liam murmured, "You couldn't have mentioned in that two-hour compatibility quiz that your birthday was this weekend?"

"That's the thing, it's not. My birthday is next month."

"I'm confused."

"Join the fucking club."

Someone handed her mom a microphone. "Welcome, everyone, to Stirling's birthday party!"

More applause.

"Now you can see by the polite look of puzzlement on our daughter's face that she thinks her father and I have screwed up since her birthday is *next* month. And the truth is... We did screw up. Last year when our baby turned the big three-oh, there wasn't a Gradsky party to commemorate that occasion." She paced to where Stirling's father stood and took his hand. "We threw a party for Macon when he turned thirty. We threw a party for London when she hit that milestone. But when Stirling turned thirty... We said nothing. We *did* nothing. That day just passed by like any other. When her father and I realized this oversight, we decided to surprise Stirling with a thirtieth birthday party before she turns thirty-one. Clever, not having it on your birthday, huh?" She winked at Stirling. "You didn't suspect a thing, did you?"

Stirling found her voice after being handed a microphone. "No. I thought we were coming to *another* party for London." More laughter. Her gaze scanned the crowd for her sister, but she didn't have to look far. London was in the front row. She mouthed, "Love you, sis."

Immediately Stirling teared up.

Her mom said, "I need to explain one thing. As the third child... There weren't as many pictures of Stirling as there were of Macon and London. I can see other parents nodding their heads because they understand. Life gets busier with three kids than with one. Or even two. A few things get forgotten. Not intentionally, mind you. But it is hurtful..." Her voice broke. She pressed her face into her husband's arm.

Stirling was crying openly when her father took the microphone.

"So to our beautiful daughter, Stirling Rose Gradsky, we are unbelievably proud of you. Not only for the professional achievements you've racked up at age thirty that most people don't accomplish in a lifetime, but for the personal commitment you made to yourself to live your life the way you want. You are an inspiration. Happy birthday, darlin'. We love you."

After the applause ended, her dad added, "The buffet is ready to go and the bartenders are here so the bar is open. And stick around because there will be cake."

Then her mom and dad were hugging her. London came forward to hug her too.

Lots of tears, lots of laughter, and lots of promises later, Stirling still couldn't wrap her head around this over-the-top gesture of love from her family.

London bumped Stirling with her shoulder. "Another party for me, huh? I can't believe you fell for that!"

"I can't believe Macon pulled it off," her mother said. "Actually, I can't believe what a clusterfuck today has been. Two sick horses, then Bill cut himself fixing a piece of equipment and had to go to the ER, the caterer was running almost two hours late, and both guys who were supposed to tend bar had family emergencies. Your dad and I have been running around like fools." Her mom squeezed her shoulder. "I'm sorry we weren't home when you got here."

"That's probably a good thing," her dad added. "'Cause honey, you have a *crap* poker face. You would've blurted everything out the moment you saw her and blown a month of planning."

"Not true!" her mom argued.

"Totally true, Mom," London said. "And thank you for passing that trait on to me—*not*. Me 'n' Sutton don't play cards anymore because he always knows when I'm bluffing."

Stirling smirked at her dad. "Got my poker face from you, Pops. Thanks." She held her hand up for a high-five.

Her dad grinned. "Two outta three ain't bad since you and Macon both got that."

"Macon didn't tell me about this party until last week," Stirling said. "And he gave me zero details. Which is probably why this surprise worked. I would've been suspicious if he'd laid out all the deets because he doesn't waste brain power on that stuff."

"Speaking of brain power…" London waggled her eyebrows. "You're with the hot doc?"

Stirling turned and saw Liam had disappeared. "Where did he go? He was just here a minute ago."

"I'm sure he's fine." Stirling's mom put her arm around her shoulders. "Lots of people want to wish you a happy birthday, sweetie. Let's head over to the food line."

There was no arguing with Berlin Gradsky when she slipped into hostess mode. Stirling vowed to make the best of it and then she'd track down her wayward boyfriend.

Chapter Fourteen

No surprise that Stirling hadn't noticed when Liam had snuck away.

He'd been damn near panic attack level from the moment the crowd yelled "Surprise!"

As happy as he was for Stirling getting an apology and an open declaration of love and pride from her parents, something about the entire situation...didn't ring true.

But what the hell did he know? He'd had exactly one birthday party in his life, the year he'd turned twenty-one. He'd downed enough booze that he swore it'd be twenty-one years before he'd celebrate another birthday.

Liam forced himself to walk slowly as he skirted the crowd. He didn't bother to make eye contact with anyone, although he sensed them staring at him.

You're my arm candy, baby, so you need to look the part of my hot rebel man.

So much for that plan. Now he felt ridiculous and he hated that this T-shirt had no pockets. Where was he supposed to put his stuff?

He headed to the bar. But when he noticed the long line and Justin and Calliope mixing drinks, he snagged a bottle of Sawtooth Ale from a metal bin filled with ice and turned the opposite direction to claim a small table in the back. No one would think anything of a man sitting by himself, glued to his cell phone.

Forty minutes of solitude ended with a *thump thump thump*. He glanced up to see a little old lady—eighty if she was a day—leaning heavily on a cane covered in rhinestones and glitter.

Then she plopped right down beside him and peered at him with rheumy eyes. "You're Sweetpea's new fella."

Sweetpea?

"That's what I call her. My little Sweetpea. Stirling is a stuffy name, better suited for a curmudgeon than a baby with her sweet disposition. My daughter went too far with the city name theme for her children. But I don't know what I expected after I named her Berlin." She paused. "I'm Nana. Sweetpea's grandma."

"A pleasure to meet you. What should I call you besides Nana?"

"I'll tell you if you get me a beer." She squinted at his craft brew. "Nothing fancy. Coors will do."

That reminded him of Macon's analogy. *I'm Coors; Stirling is craft beer.* In Liam's case it was more like...he was craft beer and Stirling was a top-shelf bottle of champagne.

Petulant much? Don't be a brooding asshole, Dr. Aloof.

Stirling had taken over his brain so completely he heard her voice in his head admonishing him, not his own.

Hard to be unhappy about that. She was far more entertaining, even in imaginary conversations, than he was in real life.

Liam set the bottle in front of Nana.

"Thank you." She knocked back a drink. "That's what I needed. Now, fill me in. You're her new fella?"

He paused a beat too long and she cackled.

"Little bit of tension, I take it? Beings you're sitting in the corner and she's not."

"It's her night. I don't know anyone except for her, so I'm letting her do her thing."

"What's your name?"

Liam pointed to her beer. "We had a deal. You tell me your name first."

"Cheeky, aren't you? I like that." She swigged from the bottle. "My given name is Petunia. Pretty awful, isn't it?"

"It's better than *Chrysanthemum.*"

"Ha! You're a funny one. Tell me another name I oughta be happy that my sainted mother *Rose* didn't saddle me with."

No pressure. He racked his brain and said, "*Aubergine.*"

She squinted at him. "What the heck is that?"

"*Aubergine*, derived from the French Catalan word *alberginia,* also commonly known as...eggplant."

"Eggplant, huh. Say it again."

"*Aubergine.*"

She laughed. "You're smart enough for my Sweetpea too. I'll bet she loves having intellectual conversations with you."

Liam thought back to their philosophical discussion of Pop-Tarts. He grinned. "Some of our conversations truly boggle the mind."

"Hey, now I know you. You're that smart doctor guy from California that my grandson Mac hired."

"Mac…oh, Macon. You don't approve of his given name either?"

"My daughter could've named him Cody. Perfectly good name and it's a city…well, a town anyway." She leaned in. "Between us? I believe Berlin and Charleston were hitting the bong too hard when they came up with that name."

Jesus. Do. Not. Laugh.

"Now what's your name?"

"Liam Argent."

"Liam. Good Irish name. Argent. That's French?'

"No idea. My father was unknown. My mother was unknown after she dumped me with my gramma."

Those eyes turned sharp. "She raised you?"

"Yes, ma'am."

"Bet you didn't give her any trouble, did you?"

He shook his head.

"Good. So, Dr. Liam Argent… What's your job at the pot place?"

Pot place. "I'm a scientist."

"Why?"

"Why am I a scientist? Because science makes sense."

"To some people. Not to me. Was your grandmother science-y too?"

Now he knew where Stirling had picked up the word. "No, but she is the reason I do what I do."

"Explain that."

So he did. It was cathartic to talk about his gramma, to remember their connection when he'd felt detached from everything tonight.

Nana sighed. "I don't get the pot thing. I'd rather knock back whiskey if I'm feeling puny. But I'm thankful that people like you do all that research-y stuff to help old timers deal with serious aches and pains."

"I love my job. I intend for what I do to make a difference."

"You will." She patted his arm. "You're a remarkable young man.

Handsome too. You and my Sweetpea will have beautiful, smart babies. But for godsake, don't name them something stupid."

He caught Stirling's scent before her dreads fell over his shoulder.

She kissed his cheek. "You trying to steal my man, Nana?" Then she kissed her grandmother's cheek.

"Nope. He's too smart for me." She smiled. "But he's perfect for you, Sweetpea." She used her cane to push to her feet. "Getting on past my bedtime."

"Who's taking you back to the retirement center?"

"Bill? Bob? I don't remember. I wish my daughter would just let me take an Uber like everyone else."

Liam seriously adored this woman. He stood and said, "Nice meeting you...*Aubergine*."

She cackled and said, "Cheeky."

As they watched her shuffle away, Stirling said, "*Aubergine?*"

"Inside joke."

She stepped in front of him and twined her arms around his neck. "Can I just say I love that you and Nana already have an inside joke?"

"I like her. Now I know one more person here. Which means, I'm up to...five people. Careful, *Sweetpea*, I might become more popular than you."

"I'm sorry it seems like I ditched you. I swear my mother would've kept dragging me around all damn night if I hadn't told her I was done so I could find you." She gave him a quick peck on the mouth. "Besides, after a while all the names blurred together anyway."

"Names blurred together?" He frowned. "Don't you know everyone here since it's a party for you?"

"I know like...maybe twenty people here."

"I don't get it. To be honest, Stirling, I don't get this family stuff." That confession hadn't been as difficult as he'd feared. Plus, she wasn't scowling at him like he was a freak.

"Okay. Try and follow along, Dr. Who."

He slapped her ass.

"My mom was mired in guilt about the missing my birthday thing. She also realized—or maybe Macon reminded her—that she hasn't been to Denver since we opened the store. So, in Berlin Gradsky's world, that means host a belated-slash-early birthday party for me, where she and my dad can publicly assure me that they love me and they're proud of me, and they're sorry. So at the end of the night, everything is fine, guilt is alleviated, we're back to being a normal family and then there's cake!"

Liam said nothing.

"Except, I didn't grow up around here. My friends from school live around the south ranch. My college and grad school friends... My family doesn't know them. My coworkers from GenAgra? I sued the company so I'm confident they weren't on the guest list. The people we work with at High Society? Again, my mom doesn't know them. I'm guessing that when she realized there'd be like twenty people I knew at a party in my honor, she just filled up the space with warm bodies from the community."

"Does that bother you?"

Stirling slid her hands down his chest and fiddled with the collar on his shirt. "I could let it bother me. For all of the reasons I just gave you. Or I could let it go and be happy that I have such love and support from my family. Not everyone has that. *You* don't have that. When I remember what I said I wanted to change within my family dynamic... This surprise party dealt with all of that. Maybe a little superficially, but it is a starting point. It'd be a dick move on my part to kick cake in their faces, wouldn't it?"

Liam framed her face in his hands. "You are an extraordinary woman, Stirling."

"Liam."

"Being around you... I see things in a different way. I learn from you. I want to keep learning things, about you, about myself."

"Okay. I'm down with that."

Here's your chance to come clean.

He locked his gaze to hers.

"What? That's an 'I'm on the run from the Feds' look in your eyes."

And...he laughed. "This is supposed to be a serious moment. Where I tell you that I only signed a one-year contract with High Society."

Stirling fisted her hands in his shirt and got right in his face. "If you tell me that you're leaving, Dr. Asshat, I will call Shanna right now and have her break into your office. One word from me and she'll set all your research notes on fire, take a sledgehammer to your computer, and smash your precious 'old school' microscopes to smithereens. And that is just the *first* hour, motherfucker."

"Good to know that you have a solid exit strategy in place for me." Really good to hear that she wanted him in her life as fiercely as he wanted her in his.

When she growled, he kissed her.

He'd never been one for PDA, but the instant her lips parted and the taste of her filled his mouth, and the scent of her filled his lungs, everything else in the world fell away.

When he finally pulled up for air, he murmured, "Happy Birthday, Sweetpea."

"Omigod, you are not calling me that. Ever."

"I will find a nickname for you, even if it takes me years."

She smiled. A bit evilly.

"What's that look for, crazy pants?"

"With your new contract with High Society, I demand in writing that I'm your boss."

"No way." He shuddered. "Since I didn't bring any gummies, I need a drink."

"Me too."

When they approached the bar, the bartenders didn't notice them. Not because they were too busy arguing. Justin had buried his face in Calliope's neck and both of her hands were on his chest.

Stirling blurted out, "What the hell?" before Liam could steer them away.

Immediately Justin and Calliope jumped apart.

Calliope brushed her hair out of her face. "Oh, hey guys. What can I get you?"

"An explanation?" Liam said.

"Yeah. We suffered through your Hatfield and McCoy routine and now you're cozied up like it never happened?"

"It happened. It always happens." Calliope looked over at Justin and he scowled. "We used our complicated...whatever this is"—she waved distractedly between herself and Justin—"to our advantage when Berlin told us to stall getting you to the party. So Justin and I acted like one of those annoying couples that fight all the time. You've been around couples like that, who don't care where they are or who's around, they just say whatever is on their mind."

Liam whispered, "That sounds familiar."

Stirling elbowed him in the gut. "So your constant chattering was part of the fake out too?" she asked Calliope.

"Oh, no. That Chatty Cathy thing she does is all her, trust me," Justin said.

Calliope whipped around. "I don't have any idea who Chatty Cathy is. Is that a TV show from the olden days?"

Both Liam and Stirling laughed.

"You guys are near pro level with that annoying couple thing."

"We've had lots of practice. But I do want to apologize about us being so over the top. Halfway to the recreation center Berlin texted me when she couldn't find your dad and asked us to stall for an extra five minutes. We just got caught up in the moment."

"I'm half-deaf from you screaming in my ear like that," Justin complained.

Calliope blushed. "I *said* I was sorry. I was in character."

"Last I checked, darlin', we weren't doin' a remake of *Psycho*."

"You are such a pain in my ass, Justin Donohue," she retorted.

"Donohue…" Stirling looked him over. "Where do I know that name from?"

"Maybe because Justin was on the PBR tour for years and won quite a few events?" Calliope offered.

Justin aimed a smug look at Calliope. "Until I got too old to compete."

"You must follow rodeo since your family owns this school and your brother-in-law was bulldoggin' world champ like four times," Calliope said to Stirling.

Stirling shook her head. "My parents were ranchers who dabbled in supplying rough stock for local events until a couple of their horses were a cut above and they jumped into breeding high end horse flesh. I was in high school and wanted to get away from ranching, so I didn't pay attention." She gave Justin a sheepish smile. "Sorry."

"No worries. Donohue is a common enough name."

"Wait." Stirling paused and snapped her fingers. "Do you have a brother who's in real estate?"

That took Justin aback. "Yeah. My older brother Jack invested in a ton of properties in Denver when he lived here. Now he lives in Wyoming with his wife Keely and their four kids."

Stirling looked at Liam. "Macon and I bought the building from Jack Donohue. Western Property Management."

"Small world."

"That's what I said!" Calliope punched Justin in the shoulder. "And get this. Justin's sister-in-law, Keely? Is part of the McKay family that *my* family has known for years. In fact, I was a flower girl at Carter and

Macie McKay's wedding."

When Calliope took a breath, Stirling seized their chance to escape. She tugged frantically on Liam's belt loop behind his back. "Well, thanks for helping my mom out today."

"My pleasure. I'm supposed to tell you that if you need a ride back to your house, that Justin and I will be happy to drive you."

Silence.

Liam said, "No, that's fine. We'll walk."

"Told ya." Calliope smirked and held her hand out to Justin. "You owe me five bucks."

They booked it outside.

"How are we getting back to my parents' house?" Stirling asked him.

Liam strode over to the golf cart. "The keys are in it."

"Yes!" Stirling pumped her fist in the air. "Dream achieved. I can totally cross *getting a tattooed bad boy to steal a sweet ride for us* off my bucket list."

"Crawl in, Sweetpea, and let's blow this Popsicle stand."

"Seriously so so so crazy about you."

"You can prove it when we're naked in bed."

"About that..." She bit her lip. "I cannot have sex when my parents are in the house."

"Sure you can have sex." His eyes narrowed. "Are you telling me you can't *come* with your parents around?"

"Yes. I won't be able to come."

"Is that a fact? Or a theory? Because if it's a fact, then it would be a proven fact with another man. Not a proven fact with *me*. I'm the variable. So then we're back to square one. I need to prove the hypothesis, which means you have to have sex with me to disprove the theory."

"Are you seriously going all 'Dr. Argent' on me right now?"

Liam tugged her against him. "All Dr. Argent, all over you, all of the time. Now let's go start some research."

Chapter Fifteen

It wasn't weird having breakfast Sunday morning with her parents and Liam.

Liam, who'd disproven her "theory" five times last night.

Five. Times.

When their eyes met, Dr. Cocky smirked. He knew exactly where her mind had wandered.

Stirling's mom refilled everyone's coffee and settled across from Liam.

The tilt of her head and the nonchalant way she held her cup offered the impression of docility, but Berlin Gradsky was about as docile as a tiger. And now her total focus was on Liam.

He'd better like things hot because he was about to get grilled.

"So, Liam. You're a mystery to us. Macon calls you brilliant, but for the past year, my daughter has called you…arrogant, annoying, irritating, a know-it-all. Am I wrong about that?"

"No. But she also called me asshat, asshole, a douche canoe, and a dickhead." Liam glanced at Stirling. "Am I missing any, crazy pants?"

The man deserved the dick-punch she planned to give him when they were alone. "Just fuckwad, fuckhead, fuck-weasel, and fucktard off the top of my head, *sugar buns*." Ha. Snicker. Two could play. If he kept this up she'd start calling him sugar *balls*.

"How long have you been involved?" her mother asked.

Liam said, "Define involved."

"More than coworkers."

They answered "Ten months" simultaneously.

Stirling's dad snorted behind his newspaper.

"But now you two are officially dating?" her mother pressed.

Liam sliced off another bite of pancake. "We haven't gone out on a traditional 'date date' per se, but we have spent time together outside of working hours. I plan to take Stirling out and do date-y type things when we return to Denver."

"What kind of date-y things?" Stirling asked, expecting he'd say something smartass-y.

"Hiking. I love going into the mountains. I didn't get a chance to do that when I lived here as a kid."

Oh, that was sweet.

"I've got tickets to a demolition derby. I take kickboxing classes at Black Arts and they're sponsoring an MMA fight. And Stirling mentioned learning to unicycle, which I'm singularly pumped about."

Singularly pumped. There was his sly humor.

But her mother wasn't satisfied. "Do you worry that after working together all day, you won't be as eager to spend time together afterhours?"

Stirling's father set down his newspaper with a loud snap. "For godsake, Berlin, give it a rest. We've worked together every day for almost forty years and you're still eager to spend time with me *afterhours*, aren't ya, buttercup?"

Holy crap. Her mother blushed!

"Besides, we know everything we need to about Liam," her dad continued. "Macon trusts him and Stirling is more than half in love with him."

Way to point that out, Dad.

But Liam's eyes met hers. The softness and happiness she saw slayed her.

"If she's half in love with me, and I'm half in love with her..." He smiled shyly. "I say we've come full circle."

Stirling melted.

"That was genuinely sweet and romantic..." A sniffle sounded behind her mother's napkin. "It's a relief to see that you two really like each other. You're not together because it's convenient. Or due to your mutual love of cannabis."

Of course her mother would be worried about that.

"Seems to have worked for us," her dad said with a wink.

"Charleston!"

"Way, way, way too much information, people," Stirling complained.

Liam offered, "Chuck, if you're in the mood for a cannabis variety that really gets—"

Stirling clapped her hand over Liam's mouth. "TMI, dude. Seriously. That's my *dad*."

A horn started beeping outside.

"Chuck, did you sit on your key fob again?" her mother asked.

"No. It's hanging up by the door."

"Then what is that noise?" She got up from the table and everyone followed her.

The horn continued to honk until they were out on the front porch.

Macon leapt out of the driver's side and yelled, "We did it, Argent!"

"Did what?"

"We won! We won the 420 Cup! The committee let me know last night. I was on an international flight so I had to keep the news to myself for ten hours. But goddammit, you did it!"

Liam had gone statue-still beside Stirling.

"What is my business partner talking about, *Dr. Argent?*"

He said nothing.

Macon bounded up the steps and said, "C'mere bro!" and pulled Liam into a hug.

It seemed Liam didn't know what to do with his arms, which was adorable, so he just sort of patted Macon's back while Macon squeezed the crap out of him.

"Will someone please tell me what is going on?"

"This guy here," Macon actually gave Liam a noogie, "crafted—and I do mean motherfucking *crafted*—a new varietal that we entered in the 420 Cup. And it took first place. *First place!* This is so gonna put us on top! Rolling in the green, baby, literally!"

"Time out, Macon. You're telling me that you entered a High Society varietal in the 420 Cup and didn't tell me?" Stirling demanded.

"I'm telling you now," he pointed out. "And the good news is we won. Liam can take credit for his brilliant strain, like he never got to do publicly with Livin' Large. This is why I hired him. It took him months to get it right, but get it right he did."

"This is why you wouldn't tell me what Dr. Argent was working on?"

"In his defense, it wasn't *all* he was working on," Macon added.

Stirling faced Liam.

Liam flashed her that sexy grin. "On a scale of one to ten...how mad are you at me right now?"

"At you? Not at all. I wanna high-five you until our palms bleed because that is awesome news." Stirling stalked her brother. "You, on the other hand, Macon Moneybags, should have told me that you dropped *one hundred thousand dollars* on a goddamned contest. I am your business partner. Partners tell each other stuff!"

"It was a hundred grand to enter the 420 Cup?" Liam demanded.

"It keeps the fly-by-night black-market dope dealers out of the running. A win is a game changer, Stirling. We can expand. You'll get your investment back in no time and you can do that organic gardening thing—"

"Yeah, about that..." She lifted her chin. "I changed my mind. I like what I'm doing now. You can't deny I'm good at it."

"When did this happen? Just over a week ago you were yelling at me for the extended timeline to recoup your original investment. You said it wasn't what you wanted."

"Maybe what I wanted was always right in front of me."

Macon blinked at her with total confusion. "You mean High Society?"

"Yes. And..." *Don't look at Liam. Don't look at Liam.*

"And Liam." A happy little smile settled on her mom's lips. "I imagine you were as surprised as we were when they told you they were together."

Oh shit.

"These two?" Macon gestured between them. "Are together? Like a couple?"

"Yes." Her mom frowned at her. "Your brother *does* know that you and Liam are involved?"

Stirling shook her head.

"Stirling! Why on earth didn't you tell him?"

"Because there's nothing to tell, Mom." Macon's laser focus landed on Stirling. "Is there?"

She stared back. Today her brother wasn't in character. No slicked back hair. No ugly Western-cut polyester suit. No cowboy boots. Instead he looked like a successful executive, dressed down for the weekend in jeans, loafers, and a sleek mock-turtleneck. It made zero sense that Macon wouldn't want the world to see him like this.

"Well?"

"Liam and I are a couple, Macon. Deal with it."

"Are you two pranking me right now?"

Given their history... no wonder Macon couldn't believe they'd fallen for each other.

Liam said, "No prank. We are *one hundred thousand percent* together. If you doubt us, ask any High Society employee. We ruled the water cooler talk last week."

Macon's gaze winged back and forth between them. "I swear I didn't see this one coming. Congrats on getting it on and all that, but don't make my life hell, okay? No mushy stuff out of either of you."

"The only mushy stuff I'm familiar with is hash," Liam said.

Stirling laughed. "My man is hot, smart, and has an awesome sense of humor. So I'm in for the long haul. I'll stay invested and help High Society grow into a better business, which doesn't necessarily mean a *bigger* business."

"You aren't seeing the larger picture, Stirling," Macon argued.

"And that's *all* you see. You don't care about..."

Neither of them noticed when Liam backed away.

* * * *

While Macon and Stirling continued to quarrel Chuck stepped up beside Liam.

Liam asked, "Have they always been like this?"

Chuck sighed. "Always. Are they like this at work too?"

"Yes."

"Actually," Berlin said moving alongside her husband, "this is tame compared to the damage three angry Gradsky kids can do when they're in the same room together."

"Kids, as in...when they were young? Or now as your adult kids?"

"Both," Chuck said. "They yell and scream and tell each other off. Then they're over it. Doesn't mean Berlin and I weren't concerned about Macon and Stirling going into business together. But that seems to have worked out okay."

Just then Stirling threw her hands up in the air and yelled at Macon, "If we're going to continue this stupid conversation, I need to reload on gummies."

"Great," Macon shot back. "I could use an entire bottle to get through this discussion with the queen of stubbornness."

"No way, get your own."

"She's always been terrible at sharing," Chuck confided.

"Family fighting and forgiving…grudges and all that is a foreign concept to an only child like me." Then Liam stiffened. Maybe he shouldn't have blabbed his insecurities to Stirling's parents first thing.

"Don't worry. You're bright, you'll catch on. If not… We'll teach you." Berlin patted his arm. "Welcome to the family, Liam."

Epilogue

Six months later…

Stirling juggled her insulated coffee mug and her lunchbox as she set the alarm for the condo she shared with Liam.

"Need help?" her neighbor Evan asked.

She smiled at him. "No, but thanks."

"Don't you and Liam usually ride to work together?"

"Usually, but he"—*was incredibly pissy about something this morning*—"had to go in early." Their poor employees. It might be a bickering twins throwback day.

"So we're on for the pool tournament tomorrow night?"

"Wouldn't miss it." Watching Liam annihilate the competition with his methodical pool playing…something sexy about that. And not just because he had to bend over the pool table, giving her an eyeful of his amazing ass.

"See you then."

She waved at Evan and then at Amber across the parking lot before she climbed into her car.

Moving into this upscale community three months ago had turned out to be one of their better decisions when they decided to live together. Their neighbors were mostly couples with no kids, professionals who worked as many hours as she and Liam did. With weekly social events sponsored by the condo owners association, they were making friends together, which was a new experience for both of them. Being happy and free to be themselves in their relationship was still mind-boggling because neither of them believed they'd ever find that kind of acceptance and love.

And hot, hot, hot sex that hadn't cooled one bit since they became lovers.

Stirling sipped her coffee as she wove in and out of traffic. She hated not knowing why Liam had stomped off mad this morning. While things were great, they still had their argumentative moments. She'd made him lunch—a deviled ham sandwich—hoping that would soften his bad mood.

She parked by the fence at High Society and considered going into the grow house since that's where Liam usually was first thing in the morning. But she'd left several things unfinished last night that needed her attention.

With Cheney doing a kick-ass job managing the employees, Stirling had more time for promo, which became a necessity after winning the 420 Cup. It had changed everything, business wise, as Macon had predicted. Most of it good, like keeping the High Society cannabis strain exclusive to their dispensary. Some of it risky, like their decision to grow hemp on fifty of the two hundred acres she owned. They'd plant one crop in the spring and go from there.

In the reception area of her office, she set down her lunchbox and coffee mug to hang up her coat. When she turned around to offer Shanna a good morning, her assistant was busily typing away—aka ignoring her. And that only happened when...

Dr. Annoying pranked her.

Sure, their pranks weren't as frequent, but neither of them had wanted to give that up, especially not after they discovered the dirty-kinky fun of making up in one of their offices.

She rested against the open doorway, waiting for Shanna to crack.

On the receiving end of Stirling's unflinching stare, Shanna crumbled like a dried bud. "I had nothing to do with it! It was there when I got here."

Jesus.

Stirling entered her office with trepidation.

He'd arranged the items on her desk.

An empty family-sized bag of crunchy Cheetos.

A stick person created out of baked Cheetos, complete with dreadlocks and a dress crafted from tissue paper, that he'd attached to the upper corner of her computer screen.

A box of s'mores Pop-Tarts and a box of blue raspberry Pop-Tarts. And a note.

A long, handwritten note, complete with bullet points.

Dear Miss Gradsky,

I am rescinding your "open invitation" to my lab—as well as disabling your keycard for the following reasons:

1. You ate the bag of crunchy Cheetos that I'd purposely hidden from you in my office because you can't seem to stay out of the bags I bring home. And you put the empty bag back in said hiding place, filling the bag with crumpled paper towels covered in cheese dust, giving the false impression of a full bag. That type of prank is borderline cruel.

Stirling snickered. *That'll teach you not to become a Cheetos hoarder.* She read on.

2. On your computer screen you'll see I super glued a mini you I created out of the baked variety of Cheetos that *you* prefer as a reminder that you should eat THOSE because you can purchase them from the vending machine here and not the crunchy variety *I* prefer, which I cannot purchase from the vending machine and have to make a special trip to procure.

Procure. Snort. He cracked her up even when he was pissed at her.

3. You are aware that Pop-Tarts don't grow on trees. Yet I don't recall the last time *you* restocked the Argent/Gradsky larder after you dusted your favorite kind as well as mine. Once again, you placed an empty box back in the cupboard, reinforcing the notion there were Pop-Tarts to be had for breakfast enjoyment. Not so.

She shook the Pop-Tarts boxes. Yep. Empty. That's why he was pissy this morning. She might've had the last blue raspberry package last night after Liam had gone to sleep. So he'd woken up early, probably looking forward to a delicious toasted breakfast treat, only to be denied. Okay, that had been a dick move.

4. I have commandeered the toaster until you learn proper Pop-Tart etiquette and issue a heartfelt apology.

What? That was her damn toaster!

5. I have also purchased every package of baked Cheetos in the vending machine. You want them? Come and get them. Or…maybe they'll be all gone since I did not get breakfast this morning.

He'd left an orange smear across the bottom of the page beneath the words:

Fondly,
Dr. Liam Argent, Ganja Research Guru

Aka…Dr. Dead Man Walking.

Stirling breezed past Shanna and her assistant yelled out, "I'll hold your calls."

The hallways were empty so she reached his office in near record time.

As he'd warned, her keycard didn't work. She pressed the buzzer like she was laying on her horn.

But Liam didn't come to the door. The chickenshit had sent his assistant Patrick.

"Oh, hey, Stirling. Umm…Dr. Argent isn't in—"

"Yes, he is. He's hiding in his office."

"I don't know—"

"I do. Maybe you should take an early break." She brushed past him and turned the corner, hearing the door to the lab slam behind Patrick after he rushed out.

Liam leaned in the doorway to his office, looking like a million bucks in his lab coat, khaki pants, and boots. "Glad to see you're finally responding to my summons in an acceptable time frame."

"It wasn't a summons, which is why I hot-footed it here."

He stepped aside. "Come in. We'll discuss this in private."

"Fine." She headed straight for the couch. "Where's my toaster?"

"I'll remind you the requirement was to apologize."

When he sat beside her, she took his hand and blurted out, "I'm sorry I ate the last two blue raspberry Pop-Tarts last night. I didn't have a case of the munchies, I…" She sighed. "Okay, I *did* have a case of the munchies and we were out of Cheetos—"

"Because I seem to be the only one capable of grocery shopping in our household."

"I know. I'm sorry. It's just you're so efficient at it. I give you a list, you get the items with no lollygagging around. I…meander and toss weird shit into the cart."

Liam studied her. "So that's how we ended up with two cans of key lime pie filling, a bottle of sriracha ketchup, seven bags of Cheetos, and a pig-shaped pot scrubber last time you went to the store."

"Yes. Stupid, huh?"

"Never stupid." He kissed her forehead. "Always quirky, which is exactly how I like you, Stirling."

She touched his face, this incredible man who understood her so well. "I'm sorry. I'll be a better roommate and throw away boxes and bags after I empty them. I'll respect our diverse Cheeto needs and not eat yours just because they're there."

He smiled. "That's all I wanted, crazy pants. Apology accepted." Liam pulled out a cardboard box from under the couch and set it on the coffee table. "Open it."

Stirling peeled the flaps back and grinned at all the vending-machine-sized bags of baked Cheetos. "You proved your point, but I definitely planned to replace your purloined Pop-Tarts tonight after work."

"Really? You've seen that kind before?" He pointed at the box.

She plucked out the Pop-Tarts box he'd indicated. It felt weird. Too light. She looked at the front and read, "Wedding cake flavored? Hey, I haven't seen this kind." Then she studied the image more closely. It appeared to be an official Pop-Tarts label, but they didn't have labels. Everything was printed on the cardboard. Curious, she opened the tabs and peered inside. What she saw had her dropping the box.

Liam caught it.

Her gaze snagged his. "Liam. Is that…?"

"Before you ask, this is not a prank." He tipped the cardboard box and a square blue velvet box dropped into his palm. He set it on his knee and curled his hands around her face. "I love you. I never thought I'd find a woman like you. I want to spend my life making you as happy as you've made me. So please, Stirling Gradsky"—he kissed her softly— "marry me."

Her stomach did backflips. Her entire body mimicked a paint shaker.

"We belong together, beautiful."

Stirling couldn't find her voice.

Somehow, he recognized that and pressed a gentle kiss to her voice box. "Nod if you're still with me."

She did and felt him smile against her neck.

"Nod if you're ready to see the ring."

She nodded vigorously and he laughed.

He kissed the corner of each eye. "Close these baby blues and give me your hand."

Stirling placed her shaking left hand over his heart, only to find it was beating hard and fast beneath her palm. Her eyes hooked his.

"Yes, I'm nervous. I've never proposed before and I'm second guessing whether I should've chosen a more traditional manner to ask you to spend your life with me."

Liam's admission of nerves calmed hers. She slid her hand up his neck and tugged him closer. "This is perfect. Way better than you dropping to a knee with a bouquet of flowers as a violinist serenaded us." She brushed her lips across his. "You know me better than anyone ever has and I'm grateful for that every day. I love you more every day. Now slip that ring on my finger before I do it myself."

He smiled and removed her hand from his neck. Keeping their eyes locked, he kissed her ring finger before sliding the ring on.

Stirling held her hand out. The stones sparkled even in a room with no windows. The emerald-cut pale blue jewel in the center of the platinum setting was the size of her pinkie nail. On each side was a cluster of pink stones. Immediately she teared up. "Liam. I..."

"The aquamarine reminded me of your eyes," he inserted. "And pink diamonds look girly on the surface but beneath it, they are tough and resilient, just like you. Every time you look at this ring I want you to remember I love you for the rare and precious gem you are to me."

And there was his sweet side. How lucky was she that this remarkable, annoying man with a noble soul and a beautiful heart had chosen her? Tears poured down her cheeks.

He hauled her against his chest, murmuring to her as she attempted to regain control of her emotions.

Finally she said, "The ring is stunning. You have blown me away with this to the point that I can't think straight."

Liam tipped her chin up. "May I remind you that you haven't agreed to marry me yet?"

"Of course I'm gonna marry you, Dr. Doubtful. I love you." She teased his lips with hers until he opened his mouth, then she kissed him with everything she had—passion, tenderness, hunger, sweetness, and most of all love. When they broke apart, her gaze sought out the ring and she grinned.

"Why the sneaky smile, Miss Gradsky?"

"I wonder if I'll miss you calling me that when I'm Mrs. Argent."

The possessive look in his eyes nearly had her tearing his clothes off.

"How soon can we start telling people?" Stirling asked. "Macon should be first. Then we should probably Skype or FaceTime with my parents and let them know." She kept sneaking glances at her kick-ass ring. "But then again, my mom will start asking things like have we set the date, if we're having a big wedding, and where we're having it."

Liam lifted an eyebrow. "Berlin will hit the planning stage that quickly?"

"You *have* met my mother, Liam. This could turn into a three-ring circus if we don't have our own plan."

"I sweated out waiting for the ring to get finished. I devised a way to propose that was personal to us. I proposed. You said yes. Can't we just coast for a while?"

Stirling started laughing. "Oh, you're cute when you're clueless."

He groaned. "All of this is making me dizzy. I believe I should lie down." He stretched out on the loveseat as much as it allowed and brought Stirling down on top of him. "Much better. Now I can breathe again." He wound three of her dreadlocks around his palm. "*Do* you want a big wedding?"

"No. Just family and a few friends. How soon do you want to do this?"

"I'd drag you to the courthouse today if I thought you'd agree to it."

A brilliant, totally off the wall—and totally them—idea occurred to her and she laughed.

"Dammit. That laugh never bodes well for me, crazy pants."

"But you'll love this." She brushed his hair from his brow. "Let's get married on 4-20. International cannabis counterculture day."

"I do love that idea. But only if the ceremony is performed at 4:20

in the afternoon, sticking with the traditional time to smoke."

"Absolutely. And let's get married at—"

"Mile High Cannabis Church," he finished. "That is perfect for us. You can wear a hemp dress and carry a bouquet of cannabis flowers in full bloom…"

"And we can write our own vows. Do you, Dr. Liam Argent…*toke* this woman to be your lawfully wedded wife."

Liam laughed. "'Til death do we *pot.*"

"We're such dorks."

"That's why we're so perfect together." Liam tugged on her hair until they were almost nose to nose. "I locked the door. I want you wearing nothing but my ring as I fuck you."

Heat rolled through her like a desert breeze. "Okay."

"So agreeable," he murmured against her neck.

"Don't get used to it."

"Trust me, I'll never get used to how lucky I am to have you as mine."

"Perfect answer." She sat up. "Now strip, hot doctor man of mine, and let's make this engagement official."

* * * *

Also from 1001 Dark Nights and Lorelei James, discover Roped In, Stripped Down, and Strung Up.

Sign up for the 1001 Dark Nights Newsletter
and be entered to win a Tiffany Key necklace.

There's a contest every month!

Go to www.1001DarkNights.com to subscribe.

As a bonus, all subscribers will receive a free
1001 Dark Nights story
The First Night
by Lexi Blake & M.J. Rose

Discover 1001 Dark Nights Collection Four

Go to www.1001DarkNights.com for more information.

ROCK CHICK REAWAKENING by Kristen Ashley
A Rock Chick Novella

ADORING INK by Carrie Ann Ryan
A Montgomery Ink Novella

SWEET RIVALRY by K. Bromberg

SHADE'S LADY by Joanna Wylde
A Reapers MC Novella

RAZR by Larissa Ione
A Demonica Underworld Novella

ARRANGED by Lexi Blake
A Masters and Mercenaries Novella

TANGLED by Rebecca Zanetti
A Dark Protectors Novella

HOLD ME by J. Kenner
A Stark Ever After Novella

SOMEHOW, SOME WAY by Jennifer Probst
A Billionaire Builders Novella

TOO CLOSE TO CALL by Tessa Bailey
A Romancing the Clarksons Novella

HUNTED by Elisabeth Naughton
An Eternal Guardians Novella

EYES ON YOU by Laura Kaye
A Blasphemy Novella

BLADE by Alexandra Ivy/Laura Wright
A Bayou Heat Novella

DRAGON BURN by Donna Grant
A Dark Kings Novella

TRIPPED OUT by Lorelei James
A Blacktop Cowboys® Novella

STUD FINDER by Lauren Blakely

MIDNIGHT UNLEASHED by Lara Adrian
A Midnight Breed Novella

HALLOW BE THE HAUNT by Heather Graham
A Krewe of Hunters Novella

DIRTY FILTHY FIX by Laurelin Paige
A Fixed Novella

THE BED MATE by Kendall Ryan
A Room Mate Novella

NIGHT GAMES by CD Reiss
A Games Novella

NO RESERVATIONS by Kristen Proby
A Fusion Novella

DAWN OF SURRENDER by Liliana Hart
A MacKenzie Family Novella

Discover 1001 Dark Nights Collection One

Go to www.1001DarkNights.com for more information.

FOREVER WICKED by Shayla Black
CRIMSON TWILIGHT by Heather Graham
CAPTURED IN SURRENDER by Liliana Hart
SILENT BITE: A SCANGUARDS WEDDING by Tina Folsom
DUNGEON GAMES by Lexi Blake
AZAGOTH by Larissa Ione
NEED YOU NOW by Lisa Renee Jones
SHOW ME, BABY by Cherise Sinclair
ROPED IN by Lorelei James
TEMPTED BY MIDNIGHT by Lara Adrian
THE FLAME by Christopher Rice
CARESS OF DARKNESS by Julie Kenner

Also from 1001 Dark Nights

TAME ME by J. Kenner

Discover 1001 Dark Nights Collection Two

Go to www.1001DarkNights.com for more information.

WICKED WOLF by Carrie Ann Ryan
WHEN IRISH EYES ARE HAUNTING by Heather Graham
EASY WITH YOU by Kristen Proby
MASTER OF FREEDOM by Cherise Sinclair
CARESS OF PLEASURE by Julie Kenner
ADORED by Lexi Blake
HADES by Larissa Ione
RAVAGED by Elisabeth Naughton
DREAM OF YOU by Jennifer L. Armentrout
STRIPPED DOWN by Lorelei James
RAGE/KILLIAN by Alexandra Ivy/Laura Wright
DRAGON KING by Donna Grant
PURE WICKED by Shayla Black
HARD AS STEEL by Laura Kaye
STROKE OF MIDNIGHT by Lara Adrian
ALL HALLOWS EVE by Heather Graham
KISS THE FLAME by Christopher Rice
DARING HER LOVE by Melissa Foster
TEASED by Rebecca Zanetti
THE PROMISE OF SURRENDER by Liliana Hart

Also from 1001 Dark Nights

THE SURRENDER GATE By Christopher Rice
SERVICING THE TARGET By Cherise Sinclair

Discover 1001 Dark Nights Collection Three

Go to www.1001DarkNights.com for more information.

About Lorelei James

Lorelei James is the *New York Times* and *USA Today* bestselling author of contemporary erotic romances in the Rough Riders, Blacktop Cowboys, Mastered, Rough Riders Legacy and Need You series. She also writes dark, gritty mysteries under the name Lori Armstrong and her books have won the Shamus Award and the Willa Cather Literary Award. She lives in western South Dakota.

Connect with Lorelei in the following places:

Website: www.LoreleiJames.com
Facebook: www.facebook.com/LoreleiJamesAuthor
Twitter: twitter.com/LoreleiJames
Instagram: www.instagram.com/LoreleiJamesAuthor.com

Discover More Lorelei James

Roped In
A Blacktop Cowboys® Novella

Ambition has always been his biggest downfall...until he meets her.

World champion bulldogger Sutton Grant works hard on the road, but his quiet charm has earned the nickname "The Saint" because he's never been the love 'em and leave 'em type with the ladies. When he's sidelined by an injury, he needs help keeping his horse in competition shape, but he fears trying to sweet-talk premier horse trainer London Gradsky is a losing proposition--because the woman sorta despises him.

London is humiliated when her boyfriend dumps her for a rodeo queen. What makes the situation worse? She's forced to see the lovebirds on the rodeo circuit every weekend. In an attempt to save face, London agrees to assist the notoriously mild, but ruggedly handsome Sutton Grant with his horse training problem on one condition: Sutton has to pretend to be her new boyfriend.

But make believe doesn't last long between the sassy cowgirl and the laid-back bulldogger. When the attraction between them ignites, London learns that sexy Sutton is no Saint when that bedroom door closes; he's the red-hot lover she's always dreamed of.

The more time they spend together, the more Sutton realizes he wouldn't mind being roped and tied to the rough and tumble cowgirl for real...

* * * *

Stripped Down
A Blacktop Cowboys® Novella

Never challenge a cowboy to a little naughty competition…

A flirty game of sexual truth or dare between best man, Wynton Grant, and maid of honor, Melissa Lockhart during their BFF's wedding reception results in a steamy hookup.

But their plans for a *one and done* change when a family crisis leaves Wyn shorthanded at the Grant Ranch. Experienced horsewoman Mel volunteers to help out and gets way more than she bargained for living under the same roof as the sexy rancher. Playing house has never appealed to Wyn…until now.

But the feisty redhead is keeping secrets and Wyn's not above stripping her bare—body and soul—to get to the bottom of it…

* * * *

Strung Up
A Blacktop Cowboys® Novella

From *New York Times* bestseller Lorelei James…

Rancher Creston Grant retreats from the world after he loses the love of his life… Can his former flame, rodeo cowboy Breck Christianson prove he's a changed man who can give Cres a second chance at love?

Unbreak My Heart
Rough Riders Legacy Book 1
By Lorelei James

Check out the following excerpt from the New Adult Contemporary Romance UNBREAK MY HEART, the first book in the Rough Riders Legacy series, featuring the star crossed teen couple Boone West and Sierra McKay from the Rough Riders novel, GONE COUNTRY, who are all grown up and finally get their happily ever after...available now from Lorelei James!

* * * *

"How do I know that you're not a shitty dancer who'll tromp on my toes or embarrass me with disco moves?"

I braced my forearm on the bar and leaned in, losing my train of thought when I caught a whiff of her sweet perfume and, beneath that sweetness, the earthier musk of her skin, Brushing my lips across her ear, I murmured, "Only one way to find out if I've got the moves like Jagger, McKay."

She laughed. "Okay."

I clasped her left hand in my right, towing her behind me until we reached the farthest edge of the dance floor.

Sierra brought our clasped hands up and rested her left hand on my right shoulder, keeping our bodies a proper distance apart like we were in fifth grade gym class.

"Nice try, but you belong here." I circled her arms around my neck. Then I placed my hands in the small of her back with my forearms resting on her hips. "Much better."

"Says you. But if your hands migrate toward my ass, you'll get a knee to your nuts, West."

I chuckled. "Tough talk."

"Try me."

"If you want to touch my nuts all you've gotta do is ask, no need to get violent about it."

She had no response for that.

Conversation was the dead last thing on my mind as I finally held this woman in my arms. She matched her rhythm to mine. Even our breath synchronized as I felt the rising and falling of her chest and her exhale across my neck.

I bit back a groan. I'd always known we'd move together like this—which is why I'd never allowed our bodies to touch during those months we first got to know each other. I'd even lied about why I planned to skip prom, claiming I didn't have the money or the right transportation. But the truth was if I'd seen Sierra dressed to the nines and then spent the entire night body to body like this? I would've had her stripped bare as soon as we were alone and I never would've left Wyoming.

"What are you thinking about?" she demanded. "Because you're making some Neanderthal noises."

"I'm thinking about the real reason I didn't ask you to prom."

"Is this the 'I wouldn't have been able to keep my hands off you excuse'?"

"Not an excuse, Sierra, and you damn well know it."

Her disbelieving snort vibrated against my neck. "I'm so glad you were able to keep your virtue and my hymen intact when you took off a month later."

I wasn't falling for her attempt to rile me, which in turn would rile her and give her an excuse to stomp away mad. "That's the only time in my life I've come close to being virtuous."

"I think you had 'virtue' confused with 'self-interest'," she retorted.

Sliding my left hand up past the nape of her neck, I sifted my fingers through her hair until I had a good grip. "You're going there? Good. We need to get this shit out in the open, so we can move on from it." I felt the ferocity flicker in my eyes, knew she saw it and didn't bother to try and hide it. "I secretly ate it up that a girl like you had a thing for me. That you saw me beyond the bullshit. But goddammit, don't pretend you didn't know how I felt about *you* that whole time."

"I *didn't* know," she said hotly.

"Bull. You were the *only* person I spent my nonworking hours with. I didn't hang with the guys. I didn't have any friends at school besides you, Sierra."

"Because you were too busy working toward getting the hell out of Wyoming to bother with any of that normal teen life stuff."

"So why did I go out of my way to make time for *you*? Only you? Because you were the most important person in my life." In pressing my point I ended up increasing my grip on her hair. "What we were to each other was always deeper than just friends."

"I didn't want to just be your friend, Boone."

"You'd have less resentment toward me now if I'd turned our friendship into something more and then left?"

"You didn't give me a choice." She twisted out of my hold and broke eye contact. "I hated you for that."

The knot in my gut tightened. "Hated?"

"With the power of a thousand fiery suns kind of hatred that a sixteen year old girl excels at. After you left, I spent most of the summer in Paris with my mom. I got rid of that pesky virginity as soon as possible to a sophisticated—and experienced—French college senior named Jon-Michael."

I ground my teeth together.

That's when she glanced up at me. "The worst part wasn't you not taking me to prom. The worst part was finding out, literally at the last minute, that you *had* cared about me the way I'd dreamed you would." Her gaze searched mine. "Then you kissed me and satisfied your curiosity so you could move on."

"No. No," I repeated, more vehemently, "that goddamn kiss wrecked me, Sierra."

She went utterly still.

"Wrecked me," I repeated. Curling my hand beneath her jaw, I feathered my thumb over her bottom lip. "I didn't kiss another woman for a goddamned year because I couldn't get *this* mouth out of my mind. I kept flashing back to that smile, the one that dazzled me the first time we met. Or the sneering one that pissed me off, because it managed to be cute and a little mean. I remembered how badly I wanted to bite this pouting bottom lip when you were being a brat. But mostly I remembered how your lips softened beneath mine from that first touch."

"Then you remember the taste of my tears, too."

Those words hit me as hard as a punch to the gut. But I soldiered on, continuing to gently stroke her lower lip, while inching closer. "And you know the taste of mine," I said softly.

That startled her. Then she whispered, "You're right. God. I'd...forgotten."

"You think it was easy for me? That I just climbed on my bike and never looked back? Never thought about you, never wished my life circumstances had been different so I didn't have to make that choice?"

She shook her head. "But it did get easier to block it out, didn't it?"

No malice distorted her words. She'd been speaking for herself as much as asking me. "It did. And then there were times when I imagined what it'd be like when I finally saw you again."

"It's not exactly been us holding hands, having heart-to-hearts, and hugging it out, has it?"

"No. But you haven't kicked me in the balls either, so I'm still ahead of the curve."

That earned me a smile.

And I shamelessly caressed the bow of her upper lip with my thumb, as if I could make the touch erotic enough that she'd let me use my tongue next time. When her breath caught, I groaned.

"Boone. What are we doing?"

"I'm pretty sure I'm about to kiss you." I shifted the position of my hand, lightly resting it on her throat. "Are you gonna run?"

Sierra's eyes were affixed to my mouth. "Not right this second. But I reserve the right to freak out afterward. So you'd better make this good."

PIECE OF MY HEART, book 2 in the Rough Riders Legacy series, featuring college-aged rodeo star Anton McKay, will release late fall 2017!

On behalf of 1001 Dark Nights,

Liz Berry and M.J. Rose would like to thank ~

Steve Berry
Doug Scofield
Kim Guidroz
Jillian Stein
InkSlinger PR
Dan Slater
Asha Hossain
Chris Graham
Pamela Jamison
Fedora Chen
Kasi Alexander
Jessica Johns
Dylan Stockton
Richard Blake
BookTrib After Dark
and Simon Lipskar